# Richard

## His Protectors

## Book 5

## By

## Ronna M. Bacon

Deuteronomy 31:6 Be strong and of a good courage, fear not, nor be afraid of them: for the LORD your God, he it is that does go with you; he will not fail you, nor forsake you.

Psalms 91:4 He shall cover thee with his feathers, and under his wings shalt thou trust: his truth shall be thy shield and buckler.

NKJV

Table of Contents

# Chapter 1

The sky was leaden, dark, and heavy with rain that had yet to fall. The leaves that were a beautiful vibrant colour in the sunlight were sullen and dull, sinking to the ground to remain in a soggy pile. The critters that normally bounded and played among the trees and underbrush just scurried quickly around or simply looked out of whatever was their home and remained safe and dry.

One curious squirrel sat upright, the rain sprinkling on its coat. Its nose moved as it stared at the large object in its path. It had not been there the night before when it had headed for its sleep. Fearful, the squirrel scurried off, pausing every few steps to turn and watch for the object to rise and come after it.

Her baseball cap pulled down over her forehead and her long mane of red gold curls tucked up under it, Raleigh Reade strode quickly along the forest path. She was on a mission, she knew, heading for her home now that she had finished her work for the night. Working as a hospice coordinator allowed her the freedom to live where she chose. She had chosen an out-of-the-way cabin where she had not that long a walk from where she parked to live. She wanted that. She had had enough of people, she had decided one day, wanting to live away from the noise and hurry of a city. Elmton had suited her. Inheriting the cabin had been a blessing that she had taken with a word of thanks to her Heavenly Father.

Raleigh paused, sensing something was off on her normal path. Her clear gray eyes which reminded a person of smoke searched the area before she shrugged, her feet picking up their pace. She was exhausted and only wanted to sleep.

Pausing once more, Raleigh stared at the pile of clothing that was smack-dab in her path. She froze for a moment, fear growing in her heart. No one should be here. This path only led to her home. Still, there were hikers who ignored the private property sign at the beginning of the trail and invaded her pace. She moved forward cautiously, her feet raising and setting down carefully. Raleigh searched the area around her. Something was off. She just didn't know what.

Standing over the pile of clothing, Raleigh drew in a deep breath. It was not just a pile of clothing. There was a man lying there, she saw, not moving. Her running shoe-clad foot poked at him, eliciting no response. She sighed. This is not what she needed. Not today. She was exhausted, as she had previously decided, the work from the overnight shift stressful and detailed.

Raleigh dropped to her knees, a hand for the man's wrist. He was alive, just not moving. She sat back on her heels, her eyes on him and then on her cabin that she could see not that far from her. It seemed that he had been trying to make it to her home but had failed. She now faced the decision on what to do with him. She could not leave him there, but on the other hand, she certainly couldn't carry him.

Shaking him gently, Raleigh heard a groan before the man roused somewhat, his head raising from the ground.

"Mister? Mister? You're on private property." Raleigh's voice sounded loud in the forest before she winced. "Mister? Can you stand?"

The man, Richard Ransome by name, nodded carefully, certain that his head would fall off if he shook it any harder. With Raleigh's help, he sat up, his eyes closing against the dizziness that hit him as he did so. His stomach roiled, and he desperately swallowed, not willing to be sick to his stomach at that point.

Carefully standing, Richard's arm was around Raleigh's shoulders as she tucked herself under his arm. She sighed to herself. There was no other option that she could see. She had to take him to her home, a home that she zealously guarded against outsiders. There was a reason for that, one that she had buried deep inside her, not wanting to face the memories.

Richard stumbled and tripped over his own feet as Raleigh led him to her home, barely able to keep to his feet. He swayed as she unlocked and then shoved open the door. She stared down at their shoes, knowing that the man would not be able to remove his. And she just couldn't remove hers, not while she was helping him to keep balanced.

Moving through the small but tidy and comfortably furnished cabin, Raleigh directed Richard to the only bedroom. She reached to pull back the covers before she paused. Leaving him standing for a moment, she ran for her laundry area and returned with large towels that she spread out on the sheet.  She turned Richard to sit, reaching to remove his shoes. Raleigh stood for a moment before pulling Richard's jacket from him.  Gently, she shoved him to the bed, raising his feet and then pulling the blankets over him.

Raleigh moved to the kitchen area, her kettle plugged in to heat water before she had set her shoes to one side.  She returned to the bedroom, standing in silence as she studied the man in front of her.  He was tall, over six foot, she could tell.  His black hair was tousled and wet.  She had caught a glimpse of brown eyes for a moment.  She sighed to herself.  She had no idea what to do now.  This was out of what she normally did.

Thanking God that it was Friday and she was done work for the day, Raleigh grabbed dry clothes and headed for her bathroom, changing quickly.  She was back in the kitchen, a mug of tea made for herself before she stalked back to the bedroom.

It was just as she thought.  The man had not moved.  She sighed to herself once more, reaching to feel for any broken bones.  There didn't appear to be any but she was concerned.  The man was unconscious. She had no idea who he was.

A thought stopped her.  She reached for the wallet that she had found in his pocket.  She felt as if she was breaking his privacy but felt that she had no choice.  Opening it, she reached for his identification and paused at the name.  She knew the name.  He was well known in the town of Elmton, running a security team.

*Richard Ransome, how did you end up here? And why? What happened to you? I need you to wake up and leave. I can't keep you here.*

*Lord, what am I to do? How do I take care of him? I need to find his family and get him home. Who do I call? I'm not familiar with him even though I have seen him at church. Lord, just wake him up and let him walk out of here.*

Raleigh was not disrespectful in her prayer. She just talked to God as if He was her beloved Abba Daddy. It was how she had been raised.

Late that afternoon, Richard roused somewhat, a hand raised to his head. He squinted as he stared around the room, not recognizing it. He shoved back the blankets, sitting on the side of the bed, his head buried in his hands for a moment. Richard staggered to his feet, a hand out to the wall to steady himself as he walked from the room. He paused, blinking his eyes to clear them. This was not his home. He had a moment of panic when he didn't know where he was.

Hearing a soft sound beside him, he carefully turned his head, staring at the beautiful lady who stood there. A hand came out to touch her curls which fascinated him.

"You're on your feet. Good. Now you can leave." Raleigh stared at him before she sighed once more. She felt as if all she was doing was sighing that day.

"I'm sorry. Do I know you?" Richard had to clear his throat against the dryness of it. "Where am I?"

"You're in my home. I found you on the path to it this morning. I have no idea why you're here." Raleigh's arm came out once more to support him. "I'm Raleigh Reade."

"Raleigh? An unusual name for a beautiful lady." Richard walked slowly away from her to drop into an upholstered chair. He groaned as he did so.

Raleigh stared at him before she headed for the kitchen. She returned with a mug of tea and some toast, setting it beside him on a small table.

"Here. Eat this. Then I need you to leave." Raleigh walked away, returning with her own mug of tea.

Richard's eyes slid closed. He felt safe here. It was away from here that he knew that he was unsafe. He didn't want to leave. His eyes opened again as he felt a hand touch his face. Raleigh had moved to stand beside him, a hand out to his face.

"Richard? What happened? I found you in the rain, lying on the path to my home. No one knows where I live." Raleigh was puzzled at that.

Richard stared up at her, not sure exactly what had happened. He could not remember anything after the previous morning. That scared him, and he did not scare easily.

# Chapter 2

Dropping his head, Richard prayed. He was not sure what he should be praying for, but prayer was too ingrained in him to not do that. His head raised as he searched for the lady. He studied her, not knowing her.

"Do I know you?"

"No, you don't. And I need you to leave." Raleigh was adamant about that.

"I'm sorry. I don't know where you live." Richard tried to rise, his strength unable to help him up. "I'm sorry. I don't seem to be able to."

"I can see that." Raleigh blew out a breath, the air moving her bangs. "I don't park here. I have a parking spot near the road and walk in." She rose, heading for him, taking his mug and heading for the kitchen to refill it.

Back in the living room, Raleigh handed it to him before she headed for her bedroom. She searched through the spare dresser. Pulling out some clothes that her brother had left there, Raleigh paused. Rori would say for her to give them to Richard. He wouldn't mind, that much she knew. She returned to the living room, finding Richard on his feet, unsteady as he was, searching for his shoes.

Raleigh dropped the clothes on a small table before she headed for Richard, a hand out to help him remain upright.

"Just what are you doing?" Her voice sounded harsh in the silence. She winced, not meaning it that way.

"I'm sorry. I need my shoes. I'll leave and let you have your home back. Only, I don't know where I am."

"You're not strong enough to be walking out. And it's night as well. You'd get lost." She turned him towards the bathroom, finding the clothes that she had dropped. "You may feel better if you shower. My brother left these clothes here. You can have them." Her hand on his back gently shoved him forward.

The door clicked shut behind him. Richard stared at it and then at the clothes that Raleigh had dropped to the vanity. His head hung down as he drew in deep breaths. He had no idea what had happened to him. He was usually the one guarding people, with his security team. This time? Richard was sure that he was the one in need of guarding. Yet the reason why eluded him.

Refreshed somewhat, Richard stared at himself in the mirror. He could see no real injuries, other than a bruise on his forehead. He had found his phone in his pocket. Unfortunately, the battery needed charging.

He gathered up his clothes and opened the door. He hesitated for a moment, his eyes lifting up. Richard prayed as he had not prayed before. He was involved in something that he had no idea what it was. All he knew what that it somehow involved the beautiful lady in the other room. She seemed hostile towards him.

That he couldn't understand as he had no memory of meeting her before.

Raleigh turned as she heard the door opening, walking towards Richard, and taking his clothes. She dumped them into the washer along with his jacket and set it to start. She too hesitated for a moment, not sure how to proceed now. It was different when he was unconscious. Now, that Richard was awake, it changed everything. She was not afraid of him or nervous at all, she decided, realizing that she was in fact lying to herself.

"Raleigh?" Richard's soft bass voice sounded behind her.

Raleigh just kept herself from jumping in fear. She turned slowly, not realizing that apprehension showed on her face.

"I can leave. I mean it. Just show me where to find the road and I'll walk out of here." Richard was determined to do just that, even if he collapsed partway along the track.

"No, you're not strong enough. I wish that you could remember what happened." She frowned at him, seeing a faint smile on his face. "You're from church."

"In Elmton? I am. I don't remember seeing you there." Richard followed her to the kitchen, grabbing his mug on the way by. He hoped that she had coffee. Tea was all right in its place. He just preferred coffee.

"I moved here about two years ago. I don't get out to church very often. It depends on my work schedule." She dropped her head for a moment as she looked in the fridge, pulling out a container of stew.

"I see." Richard didn't pry. It wasn't in him to do that. If someone wanted him to know something about them, it was up to them to tell them. Well, other than the ones that his team protected. Not that they did that much any more, training security teams instead.

Raleigh waited for the questions that never came. That surprised her. Anyone whom she had met always pried as to what she did.

"You're not asking." Her statement was just that, a statement and not a question.

"No, I'm not. It's your choice to tell me if you want to and when you want to."

"I see." Raleigh worked away, heating the stew and then dishing it up. She set the table, all the while keeping an eye out for Richard to collapse. She was convinced that he would.

"It's not who I am, Raleigh. If it is someone that I'm providing security for, then that's different. It can impact what we do for that person."

Raleigh nodded. She had heard of teams like this. She had just never met anyone on one before.

Richard sat, relieved to be off his feet. He had no idea what had happened to him, he thought again. He wished that he did. He felt very vulnerable right now.

Raleigh set a mug of coffee beside him before placing freshly-baked bread there as well. She was not surprised when he asked the blessing on their meal.

They ate in silence for a while.  Richard kept shooting glances at Raleigh, not able to read her as he usually could read someone.  She was silent, rising at one point to refill the mugs of coffee.  She sat once more, her bowl shoved to one side.  She rested her elbows on the table, her chin in her hands.  Raleigh's eyes were on Richard, almost not blinking.

Richard was taken aback by her silence and the way that she stared at him.  He grew slightly uncomfortable before he blinked.  He had heard of a lady who was like this. Caleb, from Don's team, had mentioned a friend.  He had not said her name, however.

"You're friends with Caleb."  His words were a statement, not a question.  "Don and I are old friends.  We grew up together.  His team is friends with my team."

Raleigh studied him.  Caleb had talked about a friend of Don's.  She just hadn't connected the two.

"I see.  Then, I guess that's that."  She was on her feet, clearing away the food and wiping down the table before Richard could rise to help her.  "I don't talk about my friends, Richard.  Not usually.  But Caleb?  We're friends.  We have been for a number of years.  And I do know Don's men."

Raleigh drew in a deep breath, about to speak, with the door to the cabin flew open in a violent manner.  She gave a small scream at the men who flooded into her home, Richard rising to his feet and shoving her behind him. Neither one knew the men or why they were there.

The leader of the men entered at a slower pace, his eyes on the couple in front of him.  He nodded.  He was ready to take Richard down.  His plans would start that day.

# Chapter 3

Richard stood in front of Raleigh, his stance protective, his feet planted shoulder width apart. His eyes narrowed as he studied the leader. He had no idea who that man was. Somehow it ha seemed that he was being followed. He just didn't know who or why.

"You're trespassing." Richard's voice was low but stern.

"We know." The man walked forward, stopping just three feet from Richard. A motion from his hand had his men spreading out around the couple. That was, except for one man, who still stood in the centre of the living room. Fear flowed for that man and Richard could not understand that.

"I don't think we're leaving. We need to have a chat, Mr. Ransome. And it happens today." The man flicked a finger at one of the men.

Richard heard a small squeak from Raleigh, that was the only way that he could describe it. He tried to turn to find her. Instead, he found a gun pointing at him. He raised his eyes, seeing Raleigh had been pulled away from him and stood nearby, a gun at her temple. Richard froze, knowing that one wrong move could mean the death of one or both of them.

"What do you want?" Richard waited calmly or as calmly as he could. He kept his eyes on Raleigh who stared back at him. He could see fear in her eyes despite the calmness that she displayed.

---

"You'll find out soon enough, Ransome. For now, I'm the one in charge." The man, an older man who was slightly overweight, rocked back and forth on his heels. He felt gleeful, he decided. He had Richard where he wanted him.

Richard waited patiently, knowing that at some point, he would be told what was up. He glanced at the man who was standing by himself. He frowned. He was a minister from a church in Oak City. He knew of him through Silas, his own paster.

Raleigh waited quietly as well, almost not breathing. She had no idea who the man was and sensed that Richard didn't either. She kept glancing at the minister, a frown on her face. She also knew him and had spoken with him in fact the previous week about a client of hers. Why he was here was what puzzled her.

Richard felt the gun pushing harder at his temple. Then, he saw that the gun held on Raleigh was now pointed under her chin. He couldn't move nor could Raleigh. If they did, one of them might just die.

The man paced the cabin, muttering to himself. He planted himself in front of Richard, his eyes on Raleigh.

"It's like this, Ransome. You two are marrying today."

Richard stared at him, catching a slight movement on Raleigh's part.

"I don't think so." Richard's voice, although quiet, was commanding.

"I think so. If you don't, she dies."

The sound of the gun cocking was loud in the sudden silence. Raleigh's whimper of fear echoed in Richard's ears. His gaze locked on hers, a question in both of their stares at one another.

Richard realized that they really had no choice. This man meant business. He did not want that on his conscience. And he did not want to see the beautiful lady die. He sighed, his hand reaching out for Raleigh. She was allowed to move towards him as he tugged at her hand.

Turning, they faced the man, who was laughing in evil glee. He had had his way. He would run this man, he decided, and this was one way to do it, although how that would work, he had not thought about.

The minister was forced forward to perform the ceremony. Richard wondered afterwards how they managed to get their signatures on the license application. That he would be searching out as soon as he could.

Raleigh tightened her hand on Richard's, not quite understanding what was happening or why. All she knew was that she was forced to marry a stranger. Her life as she had lived and loved it seemed to have just walked out of the window. That she was not happy about. There was nothing that she could do about it.

The ceremony was very short. One of the men shoved the minister from the cabin. The other men gathered around the couple, their leader pacing back and forth in front of them. He spun, his eyes on

Richard before he nodded.  Unable to avoid the gun butt that descended on his head, Richard collapsed, taking Raleigh with him.  He didn't move, didn't hear the low cry that Raleigh gave as her hair was grasped in a hard manner and her head pulled backwards.

"Don't deny this marriage, woman.  You will live as a couple, starting now.  We will be watching you."  The man spat at her and then walked away, leaving Raleigh in a crumpled heap beside the man who had just become her husband.

Raleigh sobbed, her nerves at the breaking point.  At last, she roused and sat up, looking around at the dusk that had descended inside her home.  She rose, turning on the lights and then finding a damp cloth to wash at her face.  She spun, searching for Richard.

Across the room once more, Raleigh was on her knees, shifting his body to his back, a hand out to touch his head.  There was no blood.  Instead, he had a large lump.  As she touched it, he groaned, his eyes flickered as he regained his senses.

"Richard?  Please.  I need you to wake up. Richard!"

Raleigh's voice reached through to him.  He shifted his body, turning more to face her. A hand came up to touch her face.

"Did they hurt you?"  Richard was concerned, seeing the pain in her eyes.

"No, they didn't.  I was so afraid for you." Raleigh's hands helped him to sit up.

Richard grimaced with pain as he did so. He watched Raleigh before he simply swept her into a hug. She clung to him for a moment before she sat back.

"Richard? What do we do?" Raleigh stared at her hand, seeing the ring that Richard had been forced to place there.

"I don't know, Raleigh. I don't know that man. I have no idea why this happened. We'll need to talk."

"I know that, Richard. I just don't understand what happens now." Raleigh drew in a ragged breath. "Where does this leave us?"

Richard rose to his feet, helped by Raleigh. He rubbed at his head, not sure how to reply.

"We're married, Raleigh, whether that's what we want or not. We'll have to play it out, as they say. That means one of us has to move to the other's house."

Raleigh nodded. They did need to talk and soon. For the night, however, he was not in any shape to walk out to where she assumed he had parked.

"My truck? Did you see it anywhere?" Richard was hopeful that she had and that it was parked where she said that she parked.

"No, I didn't. Where is it?" Raleigh paced away and then back to stand in front of him. A woebegone look settled on her face.

Richard's hands rested on her shoulders. This was difficult, he knew. *Lord, I have no idea why this happened. And I have no idea where we go from here. You know. You have our lives in Your hands. I trust You completely on this. I trust Raleigh, even though*

# Chapter 4

Early the next morning, Richard was on his feet. He rubbed at the side of his head, feeling the lump there. His head did seem clearer, he thought, grateful for that. *Lord? I have no idea what today will bring. It is in Your hands. All I know is that somehow I'm married and to a stranger. I don't want to hurt her. That's exactly what I think that will happen.*

Reaching for his phone, he sighed. No, he couldn't access it. It still needed to be charged and that he could only do at his home. Somehow or other, he had to get back to his home. And he had to take Raleigh with him. He could hear her soft movements in the bedroom. He had refused to take it, instead wrapping himself in a blanket and finding the chair again. Richard had not slept much, not when he watching for someone to return.

Raleigh had not slept the night before. Even though she had retired to her bedroom, she had not sought her rest. Instead, she had spent hours in prayer and in waiting for her Heavenly Father to speak with her. He had, during the early morning hours. She had felt reassured that He was in control and that what had happened was within His plans for her. She had sighed, knowing that she had to walk away from her home for now. Raleigh did not want to do that. It was Sunday and a free Sunday at last for her. She had planned on being in church that morning. She just didn't know if she could do that.

Moving quietly around her room, Raleigh had packed what she had needed to, closing the suitcases with a soft sob.  Rori had called her the night before and she had let it go to voice mail.  She needed to talk with her twin brother. They were close, and she knew that he would have picked up on something being wrong with her.

Opening the bedroom door, Raleigh had hesitated once more, her eyes lifting up.  She was reminded of one of her favourite verses, about lifting her eyes to the hills, knowing that was where her help would come from.  She needed that strength to face what was coming.  She could feel the doom heading her way.

Richard turned as Raleigh walked towards him. His head ducked to look at her face before he nodded. *She's made peace with this,* he thought, *already whereas I have not.  And I need to.  Lord, You are in control.  You will protect us.  You will lead us as Your will permits and directs.  Raleigh has found Your peace with this.  I need to as well.*

"Raleigh?"  His soft question had her halting in her tracks.

Raleigh blinked back tears.  She did not cry, not ever.  She needed to be strong, but this time?  She couldn't be.  Tears trickled down her cheeks. All she wanted were her parents.  And they were not here.

Giving a soft sound, Richard crossed the distance between them and wrapped her in his arms.  His prayers stopped her tears as she drew strength and hope from his words.  Afterwards, he could not tell anyone what his prayer had been.  He only knew that he had prayed for her.

"Richard?  I've packed what I need for now.  I have some paperwork and books here that I would like to take with me, if that's okay."  Raleigh was hopeful that she could, resigned to not being able to.

"It's fine, Raleigh.  Take what you need to today, love.  We'll come back for more.  Right now, I think that we need to leave.  I'm sure that we are being watched.  I don't like being out here."  Richard released her and then reached for the suitcases just outside the bedroom door.

"This is my sanctuary, Richard.  I don't want to leave it."  Raleigh was sober as she packed what she needed from her office area and then reached for some favourite books.  Her hand hesitated on a glass angel sitting on a shelf.  A sob caught at her before she reached for soft clothes to wrap it and tuck it into her purse.  "I'm ready to go."

Richard nodded, heading outside, waiting for her to lock the door and walk with him. The forest was quiet that morning, he thought, unusual. His keen eyes searched the area, not seeing anyone in the open but feeling them being watched.

"Richard?  Where's your truck?" Raleigh had not seen it when she had driven home that Friday morning.

"I have no idea.  I'll reach out to some detective friends when we get to my home. They'll help me find it, if they haven't already.  And I know that my team and their spouses will help."

"Your team. About them. They'll think that I trapped you. That I arranged this." Raleigh was growing desperate. She was ready to run as far and as fast as she could.

"Don't run, Raleigh. I'd only come after you. I want to help you. And I think that you can help me."

Raleigh snorted at that, bringing a grin to Richard's face.

"There's my car." Raleigh raised the key fob, unlocking it. She raised the trunk lid, waiting for Richard to place the suitcases there before setting in the bags that she held.

Richard closed the lid, his eyes once more searching around the area. He didn't like the feeling that he was getting.

"We need to get out of here, Raleigh." He walked her to the passenger door, opening it and then closing it when she had seated herself. He walked around and slide behind the wheel, adjusting the seat for his height. "I don't like the feeling that I'm getting." He sighed himself. "It's Sunday, Raleigh, but I don't think that we're ready to face anyone just yet."

"No, we're not, but we have to. I would rather not do that at church. I'm a relative stranger there."

"And I grew up in it. It's okay. We'll figure it all out." Richard drove away, still puzzled as to why he had ended up there. Something was triggering a memory that just wouldn't come to the forefront of his mind.

"I guess. I have to work tomorrow, Richard. I work as a hospice coordinator. I'm on the afternoon shift. It's too important for me to miss. Only, will I be putting anyone at risk if I do so?" Raleigh was thinking ahead to what they faced. She had to, she knew.

"I don't know that you will. We don't have enough information to know why. I'll reach out to a friend today. She'll start searching for information." Richard shot a look at Raleigh as she made a sound.

"And would this friend be named Emma? I already asked her to."

"You know Emma and Abe?" At her nod, he gave a brief smile. "It's a small world. She'll be in touch as soon as she has information. And that will be fairly quickly."

Raleigh didn't respond, simply watching out of the car window as they passed through the town. She was surprised when Richard turned down an almost country road towards a laneway. She knew that they were still in town.

Richard's eyes were on Raleigh as he pulled up to park, a hand out to her arm.

"This is our home, Raleigh. This is not how I ever expected to bring my bride here. In fact, I didn't think that I would marry. However it is what we did, you are my bride and my family. My family and friends will welcome you. I need to introduce you to the police chief and his wife."

---

"Andrew? Of course, you would know him. But what about him?"

"He married Phoebe the day after he pulled her from a dangerous situation. They are very much in love. Phoebe would be a good one for you to speak with. And Madigan and Silas married within a few days of Madigan finding a body in the church basement and being in danger."

Raleigh stared at him.

"That happened to your friends? Okay. So, what about your team?"

"They'll be around tomorrow. I'll introduce you to them. Then, we'll need to introduce you to their spouses."

"They're all married?" Raleigh stared at him in shock as he laughed. "I didn't know that was funny."

"It's not, but they'll welcome you. I was laughing, I guess, because you'll have stories to hear from each of the four. They were all involved in life and death adventures when they met their spouses."

"What is it with your team and friends? Can't they do anything normal?" Raleigh shoved open the door, to stare and study the area that she would call home for the next while.

# Chapter 5

Walking through Richard's house, Raleigh felt welcomed. It was a comfortable house, the colours of the paint just what she would have chosen. The furnishings were comfortable and welcoming, if she could describe it as that. She stopped in the bedroom where Richard had placed her suitcases. She sighed, thinking that was something that she was doing a lot. Unpacking her clothes, she reached for her purse, finding the glass angel that was dear to her.

Richard paused in the doorway. He had tracked Raleigh, intent on talking with her. Instead, he stood for a moment, assessing her, before he walked over to stand beside her. Without thinking, he simply wrapped an arm around her.

Startled for a moment, Raleigh jumped and then leaned against the tall man who was now her husband. She needed to reach out to her family and tell them, except she had no idea how to do that.

Richard's finger reached out to gently touch the angel that Raleigh held. It was unique, he decided, not having seen one like that before.

"This is beautiful, Raleigh, and means a lot to you."

Raleigh blinked as she came back to the present.

"It is. My brother made it for me. We had a dear friend who died from an aggressive form of cancer when he was seventeen. He always told me that I was his angel on earth. Rori made this for me a few years ago." Raleigh reached to set it down. "He said it was to remember John by."

"And you do. You don't need the visible reminder to do that, but sometimes it helps to have this. Your brother? He does glass blowing?"

"He does. Our Dad does and Rori works with him. They wanted me to come into the business."

"But God led you into something different, somewhere that He wanted you."

Raleigh nodded, her head tilting back to stare up at him.

"Not many people get that. They think that I am in a gross occupation. But I have to try and help. I was with John as much as I could those last few days. His parents and sister needed me. I could not say no."

"No, it's not your character to walk away from anyone." Richard didn't see her quick look of surprise at him. "Listen. When you're done, come on downstairs. I would like to spend sometime in prayer with you. We need that." Richard walked away, leaving Raleigh staring after him.

Richard walked through his house, trying to see it from Raleigh's point of view but just not doing that. He reached for his phone, knowing that he would have many messages waiting for him. He started to scroll throw his messages, smiling at the concerned ones from his team and his family. Then, his finger stopped at the one from Bill Butler, the head detective for the Elmton police force. He nodded. He would try and contact Bill later. Right now, he heard Raleigh's

---

footsteps stopping beside him. His phone was set aside as he turned to her.

Raleigh had hesitated to interrupt Richard, surprised to find him setting aside his phone. She knew that he would be wanting to contact his family and his team. Instead, he reached for her hand and led her to the sunroom. She looked around, loving the room. She had always wanted one at her home.

Richard sat beside her, not releasing her hand. His head bowed as he began to pray for Raleigh first and then for her family. He followed that with prayers for his own family and friends. He ended by seeking God's protection for them both. Raleigh was unable to pray, her heart filling with peace and sorrow, if those two emotions could mix.

Sitting back at last, Richard simply wrapped an arm around her. *This is nice,* he thought, *to have someone with me. I see my friends and how happy and content they are with their life mates. I have been remiss, Lord, I think in setting this aside. But this is Your timing, Your plan. Is Raleigh the one who I'll spend my life with? I pray that she is. My heart is cracking open from the strict bonds that I have around it. That is You, dear Lord.*

Raleigh relaxed against Richard, feeling as if she had come home. She didn't understand how she could feel like that, not so soon. She was quiet which was normal for her. Raleigh was used to letting others talk, listening to what they said and responding to that. She kept her private life just that, private.

The doorbell ringing mid-afternoon startled Raleigh, who stood in the kitchen waiting for the kettle to boil. She could smell the coffee that Richard had started before he had headed for somewhere in the house, just where she was not sure.

Hearing voices approaching her, Raleigh drew in a deep breath and turned. She didn't know the man who stood beside Richard but she assumed that he was a police officer. He had that manner about him. Richard reached for her hand, drawing her to him, his eyes on the man. He didn't speak at first, instead shifting his gaze to Raleigh, finding that her face had shuttered.

Bill Buckley, lead detective for the Elmton force, paused as he saw Raleigh, surprised to see a lady there and then even more surprised at Richard's actions.

"Richard? What's going on? We found your truck near the forest on the other side of town. It was pretty battered. There was no sign of you. What happened?" Bill set his portfolio down and walked around the table to pour himself a mug of coffee.

"There's a story there, Bill. Sit. Raleigh, this is Bill Buckley. He's the friend who I told you about."

"The detective." Raleigh stated that fact, not asking it as a question. She sat as Richard's hand rested on her shoulder. Her eyes did not move from Bill who stared at her in return, puzzlement on his face.

"Richard? What happened to you? I really didn't expect to find you here today."

Richard sat beside Raleigh, his own mug of coffee on the table, before he reached for her hand. His head tilted for a moment as they looked at one another.

"Bill? It seems as if I'm off on one of those adventures, much against our will. This is Raleigh Reade Ransome." Richard refused to take his eyes off Raleigh, seeing the resignation in her own eyes.

Bill stared at his friend before staring at Raleigh.

"Richard? What's going on? She has the same name as you?" Bill was confused for a moment.

"She does, Bill. We were forced to marry yesterday morning. If we had not, Raleigh would be dead. We had no choice. So now, we need to work through this and find the men responsible."

Bill sat in stunned silence. Whatever it was that had happened to Richard on the Thursday night, this was not what he had expected to hear. He shook his head, his gaze shifting between the couple in front of him.

# Chapter 6

That previous Thursday, a patrol officer had been on routine patrol. He had pulled to the side of the road, his eyes on the vehicle that sat there. It was very battered, he could tell. Running the plate number, he was surprised to find that it was Richard's vehicle. Out of the car, Leo walked towards it and then around it. Cupping his hands around his face, he peered inside. It was empty. That puzzled him. He knew Richard and knew that Richard would not have left his vehicle in this condition if he had been there.

Bill had been on a crime scene nearby. Seated back in his vehicle, his hand had paused as he made notes about the crime, his eyes raising to study the sky outside. He headed that way once he was cleared from the scene.

Walking towards Leo, Bill studied Richard's truck. He winced. This was not Richard, not to roll his vehicle like this. Something had to have happened to him.

Leo approached Bill before he walked around the truck. Bill frowned, not sure what had happened.

"Any sign of Richard?" Bill paused at the driver's side, bending over to study the scrapes. "He was run off the road."

"That's what we think. The accident scene reconstruction team is here." Leo nodded towards the officers working around the scene.

"It's not like Richard to walk away from this." Bill spun and walked forward towards the forest ahead of him. "Have you searched for him at all?"

"We've done a quick search. There was no sign of him. And I don't know of any houses in this area."

"No, I don't know of any. We'll search further but I don't know where he would be."

"You're thinking K-9?" Leo stood beside Bill, his eyes on the forest. "That's a big area to search."

"It is, and rain is moving in." Bill shrugged his jacket collar higher against the damp wind. "That will make it hard for the dogs to follow. We have no idea how long it's been."

"No, we don't. I would suspect this afternoon, but it's hard to say."

Bill nodded before he headed back to his car. He was frustrated with the situation. Heading for Richard's home, Bill walked the perimeter of the property before trying the doors of the training building and then the office building. His knocks at the house doors went unanswered. All were locked up tight. Standing beside his vehicle, Bill frowned before he was back in his vehicle, heading for the department building.

"Andrew? Do you have a moment?" Bill stood in the doorway of the police chief, Andrew McBeth.

Andrew looked up, distracted for a moment by the report that he was reading. Seeing the look on Bill's face, he waved him in and watched as Bill sat. Bill was troubled, Andrew could see that clearly.

—

"Bill? You're troubled. What's going on?" Andrew waited patiently for Bill to collect his thoughts. Bill was a close friend as well as being a fellow officer.

"It's Richard. Leo found his truck damaged in an accident out near Reade forest. There's no sign of Richard. The team is working the scene and will let us know what they find. With the rain moving in, we're not going to be able to bring in the dogs."

Andrew sat back. This was certainly not what he had expected to hear.

"You've been to his place." Andrew knew that Bill would have headed there.

"I have. I'm picking this up to investigate, Andrew. I'll pull in Lily or Jason if I need to." Bill studied his notes. "All of his buildings are locked up, just as you would expect. I don't see any tire tracks other than what you would expect to find there. I'll reach out to his team to see if they've heard from him. I do know that they aren't training tomorrow."

"Keep me updated." Andrew was on his feet, walking from his office with Bill. He was concerned about his friend. Bill had put in a lot of overtime working the cases involving Richard's four team members. It was taking a toll. "You're off tomorrow for two days. Don't work this during those days. Cora and Michael need you."

Bill sighed. He knew that Andrew was correct in his statement.

"I won't. Not unless I have to. Cora wants to head away overnight tomorrow night. We need to get away."

"Do that, Bill. We're all praying for Richard's team. Somehow, I think that he is now on one of our adventures."

"I suspect that you are right." Bill headed for his office, finished off what he needed to, and then headed for his home. His thoughts were on Richard. He pulled over to the side of the street and reached for his phone. Dialling a number, Bill waited for a response. "Timothy? What time did you finish today?"

Timothy, one of Richard's team, was surprised to hear from Bill. He grew sober as he thought through why Bill could be calling him.

"About two. Then we were all gone shortly after that. Why?"

"A patrol officer found Richard's truck. He's been in an accident. However, there is no sign of him."

Timothy rose, heading for Tate, reaching for her hand as she turned to him.

"You can't find him? I have no idea what his plans were. He talked about going away for the weekend but he didn't confirm that."

"Okay, thanks. I'll be back in touch if I need to." Bill reached out to the other team members, Silver, Stephen, and Naomi. None of them could give him any more information than Timothy had.

Concerned about him, Richard's team gathered at Timothy's on the Friday morning. They were ready to start searching for him but were constrained in that by not knowing where he would have gone. Stephen had found out where Richard's truck had been found. That had surprised them. Mae had walked in on them as they discussed their plans. She was a retired officer from town and lived across the street from Timothy.

"What's this?" Mae looked around. "Richard is missing?"

"He is. They found his truck. Bill has said where but it puzzled them where it was."

"No, he wouldn't. He can't. I'll see what I can find out." Mae walked away, turning to watch her young friends as she called Andrew.

"Andrew? It's Mae. What can you tell me about Richard? I'm here with his team."

"I can't say much. You know that, Mae. Bill is the investigator. He's away until Sunday."

"I know, Andrew. I was just hoping that you would have had good news for us. Let us know what we can do." Mae pocketed her phone before she walked away. There just might be a way for her to find out something. She would have to think about that.

Stephen reached for his phone, blinking for a moment. It was Richard's brother, Riley.

"Stephen? Have you seen Richard? He was to be here last night and never showed." Riley was worried about his brother.

"He's missing, Riley. We're meeting as a team. Timothy is reaching out to your parents, I think."

—

Riley drew in a deep breath.

"I was afraid of something like this. He's been troubled the last few days. He just won't say why."

"No, he won't until he's certain of his facts. Has he dropped any hint at all?"

"None. Listen, I'm on my way over. Where are you meeting?" Riley shut and locked his house door, heading for his car.

"At Timothy's for now. One of us will need to go through the buildings and then Richard's home."

"I'll do that. Mom and Dad will do what they need to and that includes reaching out to the hospitals and that." Riley didn't say but Stephen knew what facility the other man meant. They would need to reach out to the morgue.

Stephen began to pray for his friend and employee. This was not what they had expected. They had all planned to scatter that day, spending time alone as couples for a few days. Those plans were on hold for now. It is what Richard would have and had done for each of them. They could do no less for him.

# Chapter 7

Riley searched through Richard's home, not seeing anything out of the ordinary. He stood in his brother's office, his eyes on Richard's desk before he moved forward to stand with his hands on the black leather desk chair.

*Richard, where are you? Are you hurt? Have you gone into hiding? Reach out to us, somehow. Lord, protect my brother. Heal him if he's hurt. Don't let harm come to him that is not in Your will and plan for him. We need him back home.*

Staring down at the desk, Riley didn't see anything that would help. He knew that Richard may have made notes but those notes would be locked away until or unless they were needed. He respected him for that.

Locking the door behind him, Riley walked towards Timothy. Timothy and Stephen were with him, searching the buildings.

"No sign of him?" Timothy sighed at the negative shake of Riley's head. "Where now?"

"I have no idea. They said they found the truck near Reade's forest. I don't know of any houses that way." Riley fastened his seatbelt, not sure where to head next.

"Reade's forest? I heard that there are cabins there. I just don't know of one near where you said his truck was found." Timothy drove away, heading for the forest.

———

Nothing stood out to the three men as Timothy drove the perimeter of the forest. They would need to walk the paths but the rain prevented that.

"We'll come back, Riley. We'll search the area."

"It's a private wood, Timothy. We need to track down the owners and get permission." Stephen had reached out to a friend who did title searches. "I contacted Samuel. Unfortunately, he and Aideen are away for the weekend, not due back until Tuesday."

"Okay. We'll do what we can for now. And then reach out next week." Timothy was frustrated as were the other two men. He headed back for his home, knowing that the ladies and Sorley and Nollan would be there, helping as they could, even if it was just to pray for their team leader.

Bill had spoken to Timothy on the Saturday night, nodding to himself that they had done the best that they could. He would drive by Richard's home the next morning. Maybe by that time, Richard would be home.

Staring at the car parked near Richard's garage, Bill was puzzled. He didn't know the vehicle. He was out of his own vehicle, walking around it before standing to stare at the house. Richard had to be home, he thought, as he walked that way. His finger hit the doorbell, praying that Richard was indeed there.

Looking at Richard as he stood back from the door to let him enter, Bill could see that he was in pain and looked a little worse for wear. Richard shook his head at Bill before he simply turned and walked away, heading for the kitchen. Bill, in turn, had stared at the beautiful lady who stood there, her eyes on him, even as Richard reached for her hand. He had not been prepared to hear what Richard had to say.

"Richard? What happened on Thursday? And where have you been? We've all been searching for you."

"It's a long story, Bill. Do you have time to listen to it today and take our statements?" Richard's hand tightened on Raleigh's, feeling hers tighten on his.

"I do. I'm on duty. That's why I'm here." Bill studied Richard and then turned to Raleigh. Raleigh's direct gaze disconcerted him somewhat. He was not used to that.

"Okay. So, I guess I start." Richard rubbed at his temple. His headache had worsened but he refused to take anything for it. "I found out some information on Thursday that disturbed me. It involved Raleigh. And before you ask, we have never met before. I have seen her around church.

"Anyway, I found her address and was heading that way on Thursday afternoon, just to speak with her. I was near Reade forest when someone sideswiped me and kept me from staying on the road. I think I rolled a couple of times. I'm not even sure of that. I don't remember a lot about what happened next. I finally roused on Saturday morning only to have a man and his henchmen appeared. They threatened Raleigh, holding a gun to her, and promising me that she would be killed unless we married. I had no choice, Bill. I had to do that. I couldn't let someone kill her."

Bill shook his head.  He knew Richard's character.

"When did you come back?"  Bill was making notes.

"This morning.  I don't see that we were followed but I didn't get a chance to search Raleigh's vehicle for any tracking device.  She apparently roused me enough on Friday morning to get me to her cabin.  She took care of me enough that I was safe.  It's Raleigh that I'm worried about."

Bill asked for descriptions of the men, nodding as Richard complied.  He frowned at Raleigh as she just sat, her eyes still on him.  He wondered at her composure.  It was unusual, he thought.  The thought also crossed his mind that she might be involved but he discarded it quickly.  She did not seem to have that character.

"Raleigh. May I call you that?"  At her nod, Bill hesitated.  He was unsure what to ask her.  "Raleigh, tell me your story."

Raleigh nodded, knowing that she had to and yet not wanting to.  She knew that Bill would want to head for her cabin. She just wanted to go back to when she finished work on Friday morning and not live the past few days again.

"What can I tell you?  I headed home from work on the Friday morning.  I had stopped for breakfast at the diner.  I parked and walked towards my home.  I found Richard crumpled on the path.  I was able to rouse him and then helped him to my house. He slept for that day and into the next morning.  I have no idea who those men were or why they did what they did. I have never seen them before. As far as I know, I don't have any enemies. You'll look into my background, I know that. It's what you do."

Bill nodded, his thoughts on that already.

"What's your occupation?" He waited patiently for Raleigh to speak, not rushing her.

"I work as a hospice coordinator. There are three shifts that I work. Days of the week that I work vary as well. I had worked the overnight shift on the Thursday night and had finished for the week." She reached for a piece of paper and wrote on it, handing it to him. "I'm sure that you know the CEO and whoever else is on the board as well as my supervisor. I have been there for two years."

Bill took the paper handed to him, his eyes shifting to Richard for a moment. He frowned at the look on Richard's face, not sure what his thoughts were.

"I'll speak with your supervisor. There isn't a problem there. What brought you to Elmton?"

"What brought me here? My work. And I also inherited Reade forest. You'll find that out when you investigate me. A great-uncle died and passed it to me. We share a version of our first names. He wanted it to go to me just because of that. My brother had another inheritance given to him. There were no other children in the family for this to go to. I'll be there when you search it." Raleigh was adamant on that, Richard nodding from beside her.

"That's fair. Now, what can you add to the description of the men?"

"Richard has described them well. The man in charge? He's trying to pretend that he's wealthy. He's giving off that air. But I don't think that he is. His suit was worn on the cuff and the pant legs were somewhat ragged. He tried to hide that. The men with him? I could see the contempt that they were trying to hide. Why that was? I have no idea. You'll have to ask them when you find them."

Bill was surprised at her comments. His gaze turned to Richard, finding him watching him back.

"She's right, Bill. I sensed that I think. When did you want to head for her home? And I do need to find my truck."

"Your truck is at our garage. We'll release it to your insurance once you've given us that information. And how be we head out to your home now, Raleigh?"

Raleigh was on her feet, clearing away the mugs, turning off the coffee pot and emptying it. Richard reached to help her, leaving Bill staring at the two, thinking how well they worked together.

# Chapter 8

Raleigh walked towards her cabin, Richard keeping pace with her. His hand held hers tightly, his promises to her coming through his grip. Bill had frowned as he saw the entrance that Raleigh had directed him to. In all his years working the area, he had not been aware of this entrance. So, he wondered, how had the men after them found it?

Bill stopped to stare at the cabin in front of him. He liked it. It was welcoming. He just prayed that the experiences that Raleigh had gone through would not destroy the peace that she had found there.

Raleigh reached to unlock the door, shoving it open, and stepped through. It felt as if it had been years since she walked away from it that morning. Yet, only a few hours had passed. Richard reached to wrap an arm around her, his chin resting on her head for a moment.

"We'll take anything else that you want to, love. Or we can come back."

"Come back, I think. I'm fine for now." Raleigh's hand reached to grasp his before she turned to Bill.

Bill walked through the cabin before he came back to stand in front of them.

"I don't get it, Richard. Raleigh, why you?"

Raleigh shrugged. She had no answer for his question.

"I don't know, Bill. I really don't know. I don't know if it's related to my work or something personal. Or if it's related to Richard. That's what you do, determine that." Raleigh walked away, heading for the kitchen, where she turned to watch him.

Richard watched her walk away before he spoke.

"She's right, Bill. It could be either one of us. We'll work it as our team. We'll also reach out to those we need to."

"I know you will, Richard. It's just hard to understand why you and why Raleigh."

"I know. We need to leave, Bill. We're not safe here." Richard reached out a hand for Raleigh who almost ran to him, her hand clutching at his.

Raleigh felt fear, more fear than she ever had before. She wanted to feel safe once more. And to feel safe, she needed to be near Richard. She didn't understand that. Her heart began to pray, asking for protection for them both and a quick resolution to what they faced. Then, they could go their separate ways and get on with their lives. Only, she would not admit that in the deep recesses of her heart, that was not what she really wanted.

Richard walked through his home late that night. Raleigh had retired without saying much. He knew that she was avoiding her family. How he was to get to talk with them was a puzzle that he was trying to work through. All he could do was support her as she worked through what had happened.

———

Richard reached for his phone as he sat in his desk chair. His head bowed as he prayed for the words that he needed to say to his family. Riley had called repeatedly and he had ignored the calls. At this moment, he could no longer do that. He needed to reach out to his younger brother, to talk with him and have him pray with him.

"Riley?" Richard's voice was hesitant.

Riley was overjoyed to hear from his brother. The weekend had been spent in worry for him.

"Richard? Thank God. You're okay?" Riley wondered at the hesitation that he could sense. "Richard? What happened?" Riley's hand reached for the pad of paper and pen that he always had handy.

"Riley? I'm told that you were around looking for me. Thank you. It's a long and bizarre story." Richard proceeded to talk to his brother, telling him exactly what had happened.

"Richard? You're sure that the marriage is legal and registered?" Riley's mind was racing as to possibilities.

"It is. Bill verified it today for me. I hurt for Raleigh, Ry. This should not have happened to her. It's not fair."

"No, it's not fair. But I can tell you that God was there. He protected both of you, Richard. If He had not, neither one of you likely would be here. Now, what can we do for you? Mom and Dad are back tomorrow. They're worried about you. I had to call them."

"I know that you did.  Dad left me a voice mail. I have to call them tonight yet."  Richard's head was aching but that was a call that he had to make before he slept.  "I don't know that Raleigh has reached out to her family yet."

"She may not have.  There have to be so many emotions that she's dealing with."  Riley prayed with his brother, petitioning for protection for him and his bride.  "Are you home tomorrow night?"

"I am.  Riley has to work.  I'm not sure how many days she works this week or what shift that she's on.  I'll have to ask her what the hospice has her working."

Richard hung up from that call, his eyes blinking away tears.  He needed to call his parents but for the moment, all he could do was think about his bride and pray for her.  He sensed that things would only get much worse for them.  It had for the others.  He would expect it to be o different for him.

Dialling his father's number, Richard drew in a deep breath as he heard his father's voice.

"Dad?"

"Richard?  You're okay?  We've been so worried.  Wait!  Mom's here.  I'm putting you on speaker."

Richard heard his mother and almost sobbed. These past few days had tried him as he had not been tried before.  Being injured twice had not helped.  His body ached as did his head.

"Richard? You're okay, son?" Rose Ransome had been deeply worried about her oldest son even though she knew that he was capable of taking care of himself.

"I'm getting there. I just need to talk with you before you get home." Richard drew in a deep breath. Now came the hard part. He wasn't sure that his parents would totally understand but that they would back him. "Mom, Dad? I need to tell you something and it's hard. I was hurt in an accident on Thursday and somehow made it to a path in Reade forest. The lady who lives there took me in and helped me. That was on Friday morning. On Saturday morning, a number of men appeared, men who wanted to harm both of us. Raleigh Reade was threatened with death. The only way to save her was for me to marry her." He could not continue.

Rose drew in a deep breath, her eyes on Reynold. *This couldn't be happening,* she thought. *This can't happen to our son. But God? You are in control. You have allowed this.*

"Richard?" Reynold spoke, his voice with a wobble in it. "You're okay now?"

"I'm getting there. I have talked with Bill. We have no answers for what happened."

"Richard, you said her name is Raleigh? Spell it for me, please?" Reynold waited as his son did so. "I have met a Raleigh Reade. Is the kin to Rawley Reade?" When Richard responded that she was, Reynold drew in a deep breath. This went much deeper than what Richard thought. "We need to talk with both of you, son, and as soon as we are able to."

"That's fine, Dad. She works tomorrow afternoon. I'll see what her shifts are for the rest of the week. I'm tied up in training and I still have to talk with my team."

"And that will be a challenge. They'll back you, son. Now, let us pray for you. You will need those prayers." Rose simply prayed for her son and his bride.

# Chapter 9

Standing in the office building the next morning, Richard's thoughts were not on the team that was due in for training. Instead, they were across the driveway and on Raleigh. She had simply shrugged when he told her that his parents wanted to meet her. She had expected that.

"I'm on the day shift for the rest of the week, working in the office. I'm done about three. What day?"

"Tomorrow, I think. It's better to get it over sooner or later." Richard had reached to hug her, finding her returning his hug. That had surprised him. "I also need you to meet my team. Their spouses will want to do that as well."

Raleigh had moved away from him, reaching for the kettle. She needed to do something with her hands as she thought through his request.

"What day for that? The weekend?"

"That works. It will give you a bit of time to get used to being here. We'll work through it, love. You are not now or in the future on your own." Richard had walked away, needing to be in the office.

Raleigh had turned to stare after him, a puzzled look once more on her face. *Did he really call me "love"? He can't mean that.* Her thoughts kept pace with him as he walked away, knowing that at some time in the future, that's what would happen. Only, she didn't want him to do that, ever.

—

Timothy found Richard in his office and simply stood in the doorway. He knew that Richard was aware that he was there.

"Timothy? We need a team meeting. I'm fine, I think, before you ask. The team is due in shortly and we don't have time to meet before then other than for prayer."

"That works, Richard. You had us worried."

"I'm sure that I did. Now, we'll be done around noon, would you say?"

"Around then. It's just Stephen teaching this morning. What can I do for you?" Timothy waited for Richard to speak, knowing that he would when he was ready to.

"For me? Pray for me, Timothy. I have found myself in a situation that doesn't seem possible but is true." Richard was on his feet, moving past Timothy and heading for the board room, a hand resting for a moment on Timothy's shoulder.

Silver, Naomi, and Stephen had appeared as Richard had spoken. They shot each other a questioning look but knew that Richard would not speak until he was ready to. They simply gathered in the board room for prayer.

Richard approached Silver about mid-morning. He sat in front of her desk, waiting patiently for her to finish what she was working on. She looked up at him and then back at the report that she was working on. She shoved in her keyboard tray at last, arms folded on her desk top, and simply waited for him to speak.

---

"Richard?" Her quiet voice roused him from his thoughts. "Are you really okay?"

Richard started to nod and then shook his head. He thoughtfully watched his friend. Silver was sensing something, he knew, and he had to wait until all of them were gathered.

"I need you to do some research for me." He handed over the sheet of paper in his hand. "This man? Somehow I've run afoul of him. I need to know who and what he is. I have done some preliminary searching but this is your specialty on our team. Reach out to whomever you need to." Richard was on his feet, walking from the building and heading for his home. He needed to see Raleigh and assure himself that she was fine.

Silver followed him to the office door, watching as he walked rapidly to the house. Stephen stopped beside her, a questioning look on his face.

"Has he said anything yet?" Richard's silence was not unusual but it was concerning. He had not explained where he had been.

"Just asked me to research someone. I fear for him, Stephen. I think he's off on one of those adventures." Silver had no reason to think that. She just prayed for her friend, asking for God's protection on him.

"You do? Something tells me that you're right." Stephen looked around as the other two team members appeared. "Where are we meeting?" The team in for training had left for the day.

"His house, he said earlier." Timothy hesitated to move that way. His reluctance seemed to be shared by the other three.

Naomi watched the other three and then eyed the house. *Enough,* she decided. *We need to do this. I don't understand our reluctance. It's not like us to be like that.*

She walked towards the house, Silver beside her. She could hear Timothy and Stephen behind them. What they would find when they entered the house was an unknown. She just feared for her friend.

Richard heard their footsteps on the back porch and then the opening of the back door. He was not ready for this, he knew. He simply hugged Raleigh where they stood in the living room. Richard knew that his team would be shocked but that they would rally around Raleigh and himself and work to solve what happened to them. And solve it they would. Emma had already reached out to them, simply stating that she was sorry that they had married as they had but that they were a couple who suited each other. She and her team would work on what they could.

Raleigh heard the conversation and laughter in the kitchen as the four worked on finding their lunch and their coffee. She raised her head, to study the tall man who held her so gently and yet with such strength. He was what she had envisioned in her dreams as a teenager and who she looked for and longed for as a young woman. She had never expected God to grant her prayers.

Richard's eyes were on her even as he prayed for them. He knew the next few moments would be very stressful for her. It could not be avoided.

"Okay, love?" His voice was quiet, reaching only her ears.

"I think so. I'm just sorry that it has to be this way." Raleigh found herself wrapped tight into a hug again.

"I know, love. I know. It is what it is. God has a plan for us. A friend tells us that God has plans and purposes that we can't see. And he is so correct in that." He stepped back, reaching for her hands. "Come on, love. Meet my friends. I would say my best friends but you will be that. God has promised."

Raleigh looked up at him, seeing the look in his eyes. She nodded, hearing quiet footsteps that approached them and then stopped.

Timothy, Stephen, Naomi, and Silver stopped at the entrance to the living room. They stared at the couple in front of them before exchanging glances. They did not know the lady whose hands Richard held. And this was not him, they knew. He did not do this. He did not hold a lady's hands.

Richard looked over his shoulder before he simply wrapped an arm around Raleigh, turning them to face his team. He bit at his lip for a moment, finding the team's stare somewhat disconcerting.

"Richard?" Naomi spoke for the group.

"Timothy. Silver. Stephen. Naomi. This will come as a shock. I fear that I am off on one of those adventures that you had and that was to stop with Naomi. People, this is Raleigh Reade Ransome." He paused as he heard the gasps from his team. His eyes remained on Raleigh. "We were forced to marry on Saturday morning. If we had not, Raleigh would have been killed in front of me. I could not allow that to happen. Please, welcome my bride. And then we'll talk."

The four stood for a moment, shock on their faces. Silver moved forward, simply to hug Raleigh and welcome her. The other three followed suit.

Raleigh was in shock. This was not what she had expected. Richard had told her this is the reaction that they would get. She just had not been prepared for it.

—

# Chapter 10

Seated between Silver and Naomi, Raleigh felt herself begin to relax. The ladies didn't give her a choice. Her smile flitted across her face as the two ladies tried to make her feel a part of their group. It would take time, they knew, but as Richard's wife, that is exactly what she would be.

Stephen and Timothy exchanged looks before approaching Richard.

"Richard? What happened?"

Richard nodded towards where the ladies sat.

"We need to talk." Richard walked towards Raleigh, finding Silver rising to let him sit beside her. They found chairs around him.

Before Richard spoke, Timothy simply bowed his head and prayed for their team leader. The others in the team picked it up. Raleigh listened closely as Richard prayed, surprised to hear him end in prayer with an "I love You" instead of the usual amen. She would learn that this was his normal practice.

Richard raised his head at last, eying Raleigh as he did so. She gave a small shrug.

"It's not really that long of a story, people. But it is life changing for both myself and Raleigh." Richard proceeded to lay out what had happened, not surprised to see his team reaching for pen and paper. It was what he did himself. Each one of them had picked up the habit from him.

"This man?  Do you know who he is?"  Timothy went to the heart of the matter.

"No, we don't.  We're willing to work with an artist to see if we could come up with a sketch.  Bill didn't ask that but I'm sure that he will eventually."

"Raleigh?  You're really isolated there.  How did Richard find your home ?  And why?"  Stephen was thinking through possibilities.  That was one item that he needed answered.

"I don't know.  It's hard to find the entrance to my path and where I park.  It's hidden from sight. Unless you know that it's there, you don't find it. Great-uncle Rawley wanted it that way after his wife died when she was young.  He just wanted to be on his own.  He did welcome us when we would visit. Rori and I were the only greats in the family.  He took special interest in us."

"Richard?  That's not where you usually travel. Any particular reason why?"  Stephen took up the question.

Richard stared at him for a moment before he was on his feet, walking rapidly to his office, and then was back to sit beside Raleigh.

"This. I was sent this that Thursday afternoon.  I had forgotten it until now.  It explains why I was there."  He handed the paper to Raleigh.  "Whoever sent it to me was concerned about Raleigh.  Whoever it was asked me to check on her.  They even enclosed a description on how to find your driveway."

—

Raleigh read through the email before she handed it to Naomi. It was then passed from team member to team member.

"That name on the email? I don't know it. Someone has gone to a lot of trouble to do this. But why warn me about someone they don't name? And why reach out to you and not the police?"

"I would suspect that they know of Richard and our team. They would not want to go to the authorities without any proof. They could also have taken this route to avoid arousing any suspicion. I would think that you are being watched closely, Raleigh. And whoever it is knows a lot about you and about Richard."

"They had to have to know our information." Richard grew angry for a moment. He wanted whoever it was to pay and pay that very day. He had to release his anger to his Heavenly Father. He tamped it down for now. "That's the only way that they could do that."

"I agree. Someone has been watching you for months, Richard. There was always something that didn't seem finished when we went through what we did." Naomi spoke for the group, seeing each one of her team mates nodding.

"You're right, Naomi. You have all said that. Raleigh, I've told you what my team faced. This is likely the culmination of it all." He watched as emotions fluttered across her face, not quite sure how to read her.

"And it did have involve me." Raleigh was on her feet, heading for the door. "I'm sorry. I need to leave for work." She was gone before Richard could follow her.

Richard stood in the driveway, watching as she drove away. He needed to replace his truck but for now, he would use one of the work SUVs. He just wished that Raleigh had waited for him.

His team left shortly after that, each with the words uttered that Raleigh and he were prayed for. Richard sighed. He had work to do but just didn't have the heart to do that. He instead headed for his home office. His phone sat in front of him. Richard knew that he had to contact his family. Riley had reached out again over the lunch hour.

A prayer was raised before he reached to pick up his phone. He dialled his father's number, knowing that he would be at home at that time of day and that his mother would be there as well. He could have just driven across town to their home but he felt that he had to wait where he was for Raleigh. Richard was deeply worried about his lady. He would not rest until she was home that night.

"Richard?" His father's voice sounded loud for a moment. Reynold had been concerned about his son, even driving over to his home over the weekend without finding him. "Are you okay, son?"

"I'm not sure, Dad. I really am not. It's just that I've gotten involved in something." Richard couldn't continue, not knowing how to explain what he had gotten involved in.

"Son? Is it something illegal?" Rose's voice held concern but also love for her son.

—

"No, it's not, Mom. It's not. I talked to you about Raleigh. I, no we, need to meet with you and Riley. Would tomorrow night work?"

Reynold and Rose exchanged a glance. They had been expecting him to call.

"Tomorrow works fine. I'll bring a meal, if you wish." Rose volunteered that, knowing that Richard would say yes or no, depending on his feelings.

"That would be great, Mom. I can do a salad. Raleigh is done work by three. She'll be home shortly after that."

Richard set his phone aside, knowing that his parents would contact Riley. He just had to prepare his bride for this. He thought about Raleigh and knew that they would need to reach out to her family. He had no idea where her hometown was but he was free on Friday. Richard would talk with her later to see if she wanted to make a trip to see them. He was willing to do what she wanted.

His head bowed as he prayed for his bride and then for himself. His prayer expanded to include their families, their friends, and those investigating. He did not ask for an easy road through their adventure. He was only too familiar with how dangerous it could and would get.

# Chapter 11

The next afternoon, Raleigh paced the house, not sure on her welcome from Richard's parents and brother.  He watched her before he walked towards her, wrapped her into a hug, and then prayed for her.  She relaxed against him even as she heard a tap at the door and then the door opening.

Richard hugged her tighter, his chin resting on the top of her head.  He knew that his family was here, but he was not ready to move away from his bride until he was sure that she was ready.

Raleigh looked up at him, nodding before stepping back from him.  She didn't see the looks that his family exchanged, relief the most important emotion that they were feeling.

Rose walked towards her son, hugged him, and then turned to Raleigh.  She could see the uncertainty on her face and simply swept her into a hug.  Raleigh clung to her for a moment before Reynold and Riley moved in to hug her.  Richard claimed her again, an arm wrapped around her.

"Son?  Where do you want to meet?"  Reynold had taken their meal to the kitchen and returned to face him.

"The kitchen, I guess, Dad, unless Raleigh wants to use the dining room."  He waited patiently for her to speak, letting her make that choice.

Raleigh stared up at him before she shrugged.

—

"It doesn't matter, Raleigh. Whatever is the most comfortable or most convenient."

Rose stopped at that, her hands stilling as she stared at Raleigh. She knew that Richard would wait to deal with Raleigh.

"Raleigh, it's not what most convenient or comfortable. This is your home. You get to make the choice where we eat. If you want to eat in the kitchen, we'll do that. If you want to eat in the dining room, that's fine with us. It's your choice. I will back your choice."

Raleigh searched his face, seeing his trust and confidence in her. She had not expected that so soon.

"I think the kitchen, then, Richard. It's fine with me." Raleigh walked away from him, heading into the kitchen with Rose followed by Reynold.

Riley snickered, causing Richard to glare at him.

"I think you got told, brother, but in a nice way."

Richard grinned at that.

"I did. I don't mind. She's used to being on her own. She said that she doesn't have close friends here."

"And now she'll have more than she'll know what to do with." Riley's hand rose. "I like your friends. They'll help her through this."

"They will." Richard walked away at that, leaving Riley to follow him.

The next afternoon, Raleigh ran for the house. She had felt followed but couldn't see who it was. She was afraid, deeply afraid. She fumbled with her keys and finally unlocked the door. She slammed it behind it, shoving the lock home. Her breath came in gasps. Richard was training, she knew, so she could not reach out to him.

A knock at the back door scared her. She gave a small scream before she crept towards the mudroom. Stephen was at the door, his hand knocking again. Raleigh reached to unlock the door and opened it.

Stephen stepped inside, his eyes assessing her.

"You're okay?" His voice was stern. He had seen her drive in and run for the house. Concerned, he had headed for her, knowing that Richard would have done that had he been free.

Raleigh gave a reluctant nod, not sure on how to respond.

"I think that I was followed, Stephen. I'm not sure if I was."

Stephen nodded, thinking that it had been something like that.

"Lock the door after me, Raleigh. I want to search your car. Where are your keys?" He took them from her and headed outside.

Raleigh paced, her eyes on the back door, knowing that was where Stephen would appear once more. She was not prepared for the grim look on his face when he did so.

"Stephen? What did you find?"

---

Stephen's hand opened.  She stared at the objects that he held.

"What are those?"

"GPS units.  They were tracking you, Raleigh.  I've found all of them.  We'll search your car before you leave and when you come home.  They mean business."

"I know they do.  What do we do now?" Raleigh was angry.  She was too angry yet to let it go, even though she was aware that she had to.

"We talk to Richard.  It may mean that he or one of us drives you back and forth to work for now.  You don't want to quit.  It's too important to you and too important to your clients."

"It is.  I don't want to leave there but I might have to.  If they threaten my work or my clients, then I'll have to."

"Talk to me about your work.  Do you go to individual homes?"

"No, I don't.  Not myself.  I work at the hospice centre that we have.  At times, I am with the clients.  At other times, like this week, I work in the office.  I can speak with my supervisor and likely should.  I'm sure that I can make arrangements to be in the office for now."

"And work just one shift, if you can.  I'll call Bill and head that way.  Richard should not be too much longer finishing.  I think he was just doing paperwork at the moment.  He'll work from here if he needs to."

———

Bill stared at the trackers that Stephen handed him. He had not expected that. He sighed. He would need to reach out to Richard and Raleigh though. Bill knew that. He just had not been prepared to do so under those circumstance.

Richard paused his forward walk as he listened to Stephen. His eyes slid closed before he was on the run, heading for his home and his bride. He found Raleigh still waiting in the kitchen. Wrapping her into his arms, he simply prayed for her, feeling her shuddering in fear.

—

# Chapter 12

Bill paced Richard's home office.  Raleigh had been there but disappeared when she saw him. She was running, he knew, but also knew that Richard would find her and bring her back to speak with him.

"Richard?  You searched her car?"

"I did.  This morning before she left."  Richard rubbed at his cheek.  "It has to have been placed at her work."

"That would make sense. I need to talk with her. Will she come back?"  Bill looked towards the door.

"She will.  Just give her a moment or two." Richard sat, pointing to a chair.  "Where does the investigation stand, Bill?"

"About there.  We haven't any word on a name for the men.  There was no evidence on your truck. We didn't know about Raleigh's home in time to go through it."

"And you would not have found anything, Bill." Raleigh had returned.  "We cleaned before we left.  I wasn't thinking of that at all.  I guess that I should have."

"We not likely would have found anything much.  Talk to me, Raleigh, in general terms about your work."

"My work?  I'm a coordinator for hospice services.  I arrange for workers to be paired with those in hospice. That can be at the hospice itself or in their home. On occasion, I take a shift. That's not common. I also find volunteers and paid staff and arrange for their training. It's a complicated task that I have."

"It sounds like it. Do you know of anyone who might have a grudge against you because of a client?"

Raleigh shrugged, having thought back through the clients who she had dealt with.

"I really don't know, Bill. There may be. I can't give you the names. You would need a warrant for that. It's confidential."

"I understand that. If we need to, then we will. I'll speak with your supervisor as well to ascertain if there are any issues with any of the other staff. They should be able to give general information on that."

"There has been a turnover in the last six months. It's stressful what we do. It causes burn-out. We try and provide counselling for those who want it. It is rewarding in itself, our work, in providing comfort to the client and their families."

"I can see that. It is, unfortunately, a needed service." Bill stood, his eyes on the dark oak hardwood floor. "If you think of anything, call me. If you find that you are being followed, head for our department and head inside. One of our officers will escort you home. And Richard and his team will do the same. You are not alone in this, Raleigh. Neither is Richard. We have a vast group of friends who had undergone something like this. If you need to, ask Richard who you can talk to."

"Thank you for your concern, Bill. I have reached out to some friends. They know only too well what this is like." Raleigh had not thought to say that her hometown was Riverville.

Richard waited as Bill drove away before he reached for Raleigh, drawing her down into his favourite seat on the front porch. Night was dropping down, the stars and moon playing hide and seek with the clouds.

"Lots of friends? Where are you from, Raleigh? I don't know that we've talked about that."

Raleigh shifted how she was sitting, leaning back against him. Her prayer was that he stayed safe but also that he never left her.

"I'm from Riverville. And I would suspect that Abe is a good friend of yours."

"He is. But you have other friends there."

"I do. Darci is a good friend. I've been talking with her. And Frankie's Deirdre is as well. I know what that group all went through."

"They went through what my friends went through. We'll talk, love. We'll talk. We may also need to start making plans on how to keep you safe."

"Include yourself in that. You're in danger too, Richard. I just wish I knew why. I have no idea who that man was or why." Raleigh grew silent, her thoughts troubled before she turned her mind to the verses that spoke of protection and peace.

"I have. My team is working on that. It may mean that we hide out somewhere."

"That's not you, Richard. You need to be at the forefront leading the charge. It may come to you stepping back and letting others lead the charge."

"It may." Richard grew silent, content to hold his lady. His thoughts too turned to prayer, confident that he was being heard.

The men skirting the woods near the house dared not move in any closer. They had tried that, only to find out that Richard had good security in place, including motion sensor lights near the edge of the property. They didn't want to risk setting one of them off. They argued before they made their way back to their car.

Richard rose at last, tugging Raleigh to her feet. It was late and the morning came early, too early he thought. He kissed her temple and sent her to her rest. He would work for a while longer, he decided, instead reaching for his Bible.

# Chapter 13

Richard hit his hands and knees, the brutal blow to his back driving him down. He reached awkwardly to feel at his back, finding instead that he was flat on his face. He could feel a heavy boot grinding into his lower back and another foot holding his wrist to the ground. Richard had headed for his training building after Raleigh had left for work, intending on working out for a bit before the trainees arrived. He had not expected to be attacked.

His attackers remained silent. He felt the blows that he took, his body absorbing the hits before a chance blow hit his head. His senses blackened as he lost his fight to stay conscious.

An hour later, he felt hands on him, assessing him and then lifting him. He lost the fight once more and didn't feel the stretcher move as it was wheeled towards the ambulance. Richard's team had found him, the trainees standing in shocked silence watching.

Naomi headed the trainees into the training building, Timothy with her. Stephen rode with Richard. Silver had taken a look at Richard and then ran for her car. She needed to find Raleigh. Raleigh needed to be with Richard.

Raleigh raised her head from her work as she heard her supervisor speaking to her, telling her that someone was there to speak with her. She was on her feet, expecting to see Bill. She had not expected to see Silver.

"Silver? Why are you here?" Raleigh's face paled before she was back in her office, grabbing her purse, and then finding her supervisor. Back with Silver, Raleigh simply headed for the door. "How bad?"

"We don't know." Silver pointed to her car. "We'll grab your car later. Right now, you need to be with Richard. He's not conscious. We found him near the training building."

"He was heading there this morning after I left. He said something about a work out." Raleigh withdrew after saying that, her eyes on the passing scenery.

Silver stayed close to Raleigh, her eyes on the move. She found Stephen waiting for them, a hand out to draw Raleigh to one side.

"Stephen? How is he?"

"They're working on him, Raleigh. He was beaten. We just don't know how badly as yet." He shoved her down into a chair, Silver nodding as she stood nearby, her eyes still in constant motion.

"It must have been after I left. He was heading for a work out. I want these men. And I want them yesterday." Raleigh was fierce in her words.

Stephen gave a quick grin at her words. She was angry, he knew, that Richard had been hurt. He had put in a call to Bill, who had responded from yet another crime scene. It was almost too much, Stephen thought, for the squad of detectives.

Bill walked through the ambulance bay doors, heading for the charge nurse. A quiet word with her and Bill headed for an examination room. He stood for a moment, watching as Richard was assessed and heard his friend speaking, his voice filled with pain.

When he could, Bill approached Richard. A hand rested on the siderail to the bed.

"Richard, what can you tell me?"

"Absolutely nothing. I was down before I could even realize that someone was there." Richard squinted at Bill, one eye closed against the light. "Raleigh?"

"She's with Stephen and Silver in the waiting room. We need to investigate her further."

"I know that you do. Talk to Frankie Brennan in Riverville. His wife is her friend. That's also her hometown." Richard knew the couple as well. Frankie was the lead detective on that town's police force.

"Riverville? Wonderful. We'll find out what we need then without too much of a hassle. I'll leave and let her come in. You need to watch yourself, my friend. We don't know who or why."

"I know that." Richard looked past Bill, seeing Raleigh hesitating in the doorway. A hand stretched out for her. "Come here, love. It's okay for you to be here."

Raleigh almost threw herself at Richard. Her fear when Silver had appeared was that Richard was critically injured or even dead. She was wrapped in his arms, not hearing the groan that he gave.

—

The emergency room physician nodded at Bill as he entered the room. He paused for a moment before he set the chart on the bedside table. Raleigh stood back as he examined Richard. The physician stood, hands on the end of the bed, assessing Richard. He knew Richard from his work around town.

"Who did this to you, Richard? And it's not the first time in the last week that you have ended up unconscious."

"No, unfortunately it's not." Richard concisely described his other injuries.

"I doubt that you had a concussion before but being knocked out three times? That's pushing it, my friend. This is your wife?"

"It is. Her name is Raleigh."

"Raleigh, we need to watch Richard carefully over the next day or so. He's not to work. No computers. He needs to rest. Can you ensure that he does that?"

Richard watched as Raleigh didn't reply. He guessed that she was thinking through her work, deciding what she could do.

"I can do that. I'll speak with my supervisor. If someone can retrieve some work for me, I can work from home. That's not a problem." Raleigh turned as Silver spoke from beside her. "Silver?"

"I know her and she knows what I do. That won't be a problem. I'll head that way. Stephen will come with me and retrieve your car. Timothy will be here to drive you home. That's not an option."

Silver walked away, leaving Raleigh turning back to Richard, who simply nodded. His team was doing what they were trained to do. He didn't need to worry. They would be taken care of. That was all that mattered.

Late that night, Richard finally slept. His body hurt but not as much as his heart was hurting. His bride had been scared again. He wanted to spare her that. It just hadn't worked out that way.

Raleigh curled up on her bed, a blanket drawn over her. She would not sleep, she knew. She would be on her feet, checking on Richard over the night whether he knew it or not. That was what her training was.

Silver had delivered her work to her, simply stating that her supervisor understood and simply asked that Raleigh call her in the morning. Stephen had handed her the keys to her car, a stern look on his face that softened as he grinned at her and told her the car was clean.

Raleigh had thanked them. They were doing what they were paid to do. Only, it went beyond that. They considered her a friend, not just their employer's wife. She felt that she was a part of the group here, something that had been missing for the last couple of years.

Her thoughts turned to prayer. She prayed as she had never prayed in the past, knowing that God was watching over them. It could have been so much worse for Richard, she acknowledged. *Lord, how long? How many times will Richard be hurt because of me? Or is*

Raleigh's thoughts grew quiet as she slept. Richard was up and down instead checking on his bride.  He stood for a few moments, his eyes on her, as he prayed for her.  He could feel danger moving in on both of them, like a huge circling tornado.  He just didn't know if they would survive.

He sat on the side of his bed, his head dropping. He was hurting and tired.  He just wished he could end it all that night, find the ones responsible, and then live life with the bride of his dreams.

—

# Chapter 14

Richard's head turned the next morning as he heard a tap at the back door and then the door opening. Silver and Stephen stood there, knowing that Timothy and Naomi had headed for the training building. That pair were on duty that day and would explain that Richard would be teaching the end of the training session.

Raleigh looked around from where she stood in the kitchen doorway. She turned and walked away, heading for Richard's office. Work was waiting for her as much as she didn't want to work.

Richard watched her walk away before he spoke, not turning his head this time. Silver poured their coffee, setting it on the table before she walked after Raleigh. She stood for a moment before she approached her.

"Raleigh? What can we do for you?"

Silver's question didn't surprise Raleigh. It was what she had come to expect from the team. Raleigh shrugged, not sure what to say.

"Okay, I guess, Silver. I just wish this had never happened." She looked down at her work, knowing that it was waiting for her, except that she just didn't think that she could work that day. "How do we solve this, Silver? I know that's what you do on the team."

Silver nodded. Raleigh was reacting as she had expected her to; it was sooner than she thought that she would.

—

"We start with looking at both your families. Richard's family we know quite well. But we have to research that, their families and friends. Then we look at your family, friends, that kind of thing. We look at your education. With Naomi, it was a former classmate and his father that went after Nollan and her."

"That's a lot." Raleigh bit at her lip before she reached for her phone. She sent a text message off to her supervisor, asking for the day. She noted that she would work on her duties as she could that day. The response was swift, her supervisor simply agreed and told Raleigh that they were in her prayers.

Silver had waited, hearing the conversation in the kitchen. She frowned as Raleigh did not set aside her phone but sent more text messages.

Raleigh looked up after some minutes, a thoughtful look on her face. She had set an investigation in process. She just was not sure that what she had done was the right thing.

"I'm sorry. Silver, I have reached out to some friends. You would know that I am from Riverville. Richard has mentioned that you are friends with Abe's team. So am I. I have asked Micah's Kat to start a search on both our family trees. Emma has already started her investigation but has been pulled away because of urgent investigations. She has employees that will work it for her."

Silver stared at her for a moment before she just reached to hug her. This was wonderful news, she

—

decided.   Maybe, just maybe, they could stop this before it went too far.

"And Richard is aware of this?"  Silver looked up to see the two men standing beside her.

Richard   nodded,   having   heard   their conversation.

"I am.  And I am thankful for Raleigh's friends. We've worked together before.  Now, Raleigh, you need to work."  He stared at her as she shook her head. "You don't?"

"No, I don't.  I can work with you today, but I may need to pull back to do some of my own work. Where do we start?"  Raleigh was on her feet, moving from his desk chair.  Richard simply wrapped her in a hug.

"We start as we always do, listing everyone who we know that we can name.  With our occupations, Raleigh, there will be names that we cannot give.  Bill, if he needs them, will need search warrants for those."

Raleigh simply reached for a pad of paper and became to write, not even bothering to find a seat. Silver and Stephen stared at her for a moment before Richard shove her into a chair. He was learning that when Raleigh wanted to do something, she just did it, without thought for her comfort.  Raleigh's soft thank you surprised the other two in the room.

Silver shook her head at Richard, seeing his grin at her.  She tilted her head for a moment before nodding.  Richard, while still intense, was relaxing.

Raleigh had done that. She made a mental note to thank her.

Stephen turned from Richard, heading for a storage closet and returning with rolls of paper. Silver moved to help him remove pictures from the wall and then tape the paper to the walls. It would stay there for as long as they needed it to.

Riley stood for a moment, studying the activity in the room. He walked towards his brother, finding him sitting with his eyes closed. Richard had a look of pain on his face, but Riley knew that he would just refuse to leave the room.

"Richard?" Riley's voice was soft, but Richard turned towards him. "What are you four up to?"

"Research. Investigation. It's what we do." Richard sighed as he levered himself to his feet, waiting for his head to clear. "I need to head to the training building. They're almost done for the day."

"Come on then, Richard. I'll walk you out there." Riley walked away with Richard, not seeing Raleigh's head raising as she watched them walk away.

"It's okay, Raleigh." Stephen spoke without looking up. "He always shows up at the end of a training session, just to assess the trainees and answer any questions that they may have. Riley will make sure that he doesn't overdo it. So will Naomi and Timothy. He doesn't relax when we have trainees in."

"And he needs to. How can he heal if he doesn't?" Raleigh's question didn't require an answer. She was just putting it out there.

Silver rose at last, walking around the room, reading the names. She was surprised at how many names were shared with all of them.

"Stephen? Did you notice this?" She turned to find the other two watching her closely.

"Notice what?" He frowned at Silver. She had interrupted him just as a thought had come to him. He scribbled it down as he waited for her to respond.

"That there are so many names in common between Richard and Raleigh. And we know many of them."

Raleigh's hand paused, poised in the air as she stopped her writing. She frowned at Silver in turn, before she was on her feet, following Silver's steps.

"We do have a number in common. So, we eliminate who we can and add as we learn more."

Stephen and Silver nodded at one another. Raleigh had quickly picked up on what was the norm for them. Silver turned once more as she heard Timothy's voice, not surprised to find Tate with him.

"Where do we stand?" Timothy's question broke through the silence.

"In Richard's office, trying to make sense of how we all know so many of the same people." Raleigh's quiet comment startled them before they began to laugh, drawing a questioning look from the three who had just entered the room.

———

# Chapter 15

Walking through the yard that afternoon, Raleigh was on a mission as her brother would have said. She headed for the training building, not knowing that Richard walked beside her. She jumped as she felt him take her hand

"Richard? You're supposed to be resting." She tried to turn them back towards the house.

"No, I'm okay, love. It's fine. You're wanting a tour?"

"I am. At least, I was. I never thought that the buildings would be locked." She looked down at the keys which he held in his extended hand. "Richard? What's this?"

"Keys to the buildings, love. It's your home area. Even though these are work buildings, you are still welcome to enter them. I will not stop you. In fact, it's likely a good idea that you are familiar with them." Richard stared into the distance for a moment. "Raleigh, you teach the volunteers, don't you?"

"I do. Why?"

"Because sometimes we have people who have terminal diseases that we need to provide security for. It has been difficult, not knowing what to do or say. Your experience would help us with that."

Raleigh nodded, knowing what he was asking.

"You want me to come up with teaching material and train you in that."

—

"That would work. But what I really had in mind was for you to teach it." Richard waited as she thought it through, watching her walk the training building, including the exercise room.

"I would need to pray about that. Abe has asked me the same thing. I refused him just because of how far the travel would be. I mean, it's not that far but this would take from me."

"It would. We'll pray about it before we say anything to anyone else." Richard reached for her hand, locking the door behind them. "We'll tour the office building next."

"This is a nice area, Richard. I like your landscaping. But I am afraid with the trees so close." Raleigh shivered as she stared around, feeling them watched. "Someone is out there."

"There is. We've seen evidence of them on the ground and found someone moving around just far enough away from the cameras so that we can't identify them."

"I see." Raleigh walked through the office building, liking it. "Whoever designed this thought ahead."

"Thank you, love. I had the thoughts and a friend drew the plans for me. If you see something that you think might need updating, let me know." He stopped at the office next to his own, flipping on the lights. "If you do decide to work with us, this would be your office. I had an extra one designed when I built, not knowing if I would bring in someone else. The other four have their own offices. Tate and Shanli are in and out, helping with the paperwork and whatnot.”

“You have created a nice building. Your team? I can’t describe how welcome that they have made me.” Raleigh walked into his hug.

“Thank you, love.” Richard stood for a moment, holding the lady who was claiming his heart in a fast and furious way. “Now, your family? Are they home on the weekend?”

“They are.” She tilted her head back to look up at him. “Why?”

“Because I think we need to take a road trip back to your town. It’s not that far. We need to meet with them. I know that we have spoken with them, but it’s not the same.”

“No, it’s not. They need to meet you face to face.” Raleigh bit at her lip, suddenly uncertain about his reception with her family.

“It’s okay, love. We’ll go and meet with them. I can take what they dish out.” Richard grinned at her stare.

“And to be sure, Rori will. He’s very protective of me. That’s what twins do.” Raleigh walked away from him, stopping outside to wait as he locked up.

“I’m taking you out for a meal, Raleigh. We can’t hide. It never works. If it comes to a time when we do need to, Naomi will have sourced out houses for us to use. That time hasn’t come yet.”

“That’s what I’m afraid of, Richard. We’ll have to go into hiding and that will disrupt your training

——

schedule. And I know from my friends that it really doesn't work." Raleigh climbed up into the cab of Richard's new truck, fastening her seatbelt. She was more worried than she wanted to admit.

Richard started the truck and then bowed his head to pray before he drove off. He was still somewhat hesitant to drive, not knowing exactly what had happened to him. His hand reached for Raleigh's, finding her fingers curling around his.

Ev, Andrew's aunt, made her way through her diner, greeting friend and stranger alike, as she moved towards Richard. She frowned for a moment before she recognized Raleigh. She was puzzled to see the two of them together. Neither dated, that much she knew.

"Richard? Raleigh? You're together?" Ev was not prying, they both knew.

"We are. Ev, have a seat." Richard waited as Raleigh shifted over to let Ev sit beside her. "I, no we, need your help. We're off on one of those adventures that we told Naomi was to stop with her. I won't go into all the details, not here in the diner, but Raleigh and I are married. It would have meant her life if we hadn't. I'll let you put it out if anyone asks."

"And they will. People in this town know you, Richard, and know that you don't date. To see you with Raleigh? That will raise speculation. We'll make sure the word gets out. And Avery is here today. I'll send him out to talk with you." Ev was away with their orders, leaving Raleigh staring after her in shock.

Richard laughed, bringing her eyes to him.

—

88

"That's Ev. She's like that. And in case you missed it, she's Andrew's aunt." Richard paused for a moment to let Raleigh absorb that. "And her son, Avery, is in law enforcement as well. He'll work this for us from his perspective."

"We're disturbing so many people with this." Raleigh looked up with a word of thanks as mugs of coffee appeared in front of them.

"We are, but they all will help us. That's how our town works. And that's how your town works as well. I am sure that Bill has reached out to Frankie."

"I'm sure that he has. And if he has, then Frankie will talk to Abe. And Abe will talk to his team. And then the team will want to lock me away." She looked up. "Emma has a cousin in town."

Richard's hand paused as he reached for his mug before he nodded.

"Jonah's Candace. We'll need to get that group together with us. I have a large circle of friends."

"That's what I'm afraid of. I'll be swamped with people. I don't know if I can do that."

Richard was grinning at her words.

"You'll be fine. They're all a great group. We can take it in stages if you feel better."

"And then some will feel left out. No, just set it up. But when you're better. For now, it's enough that you're meeting my family. And then we have the meal with your team on Sunday." Raleigh's thoughts drifted away from the diner and back towards her home. She missed it.

# Chapter 16

That Saturday, Richard slowed to drive along the main street of Riverville. It had been a number of months since he had been in the town. He watched Raleigh carefully, assessing her for any stress. She was relaxed, he saw, interest on her face.

"I want to stop at Rylee's bakeshop, Richard. I need some of her Irish baking."

"We can do that." He pulled into a parking spot in front of the bakeshop.

"How be we do that now, just in case we're late leaving your folks? I don't want to rush you away from them."

"Thank you, Richard. Not many people think of that." She waited for him to help her from the truck, her hand tucked tight in his as they approached the shop. She turned as she heard her name. "Dave? You're not working today?"

Dave Allison, a town paramedic, shook his head. He had been running errands and was now heading to find his wife, Rylee.

"No, I'm not." He hugged Raleigh. "You're in town? It's been a while." His voice held the questions that he would not ask.

"I am. We're here to visit my folks." She bit at her lip for a moment. "You know Richard?"

"I do." Dave studied Richard, not sure why they were together.

———

"It will get out soon, Dave.  Richard and I have married under circumstances that were forced on us."

Dave's face grew stern.  Having gone through a very dangerous adventure with Rylee, Dave had a good idea of what Raleigh was not saying.

"Forced?"

Raleigh nodded, not willing to say why.  Richard watched her before he spoke.

"It was that or Raleigh's life.  I couldn't say no, Dave.  And Abe is aware of it, in case you're wondering."

"I wondered."  He pulled open the door, the aroma of fresh baking and spices floating out. "Come on in. Rylee will want to see you."

Rylee watched thirty minutes later as Richard drove away, Dave's arm around her.

"She's in danger, Dave."

"She is.  All we can do is pray for them. And maybe take a drive over there."

Richard drew to a stop at the curb in front of the home where Raleigh had grown up.  He liked the look of the neat brick bungalow.  His hand reached for her, his head bowing in prayer for them. *Lord, I have no idea what to expect, what sort of welcome I'll receive. You are here.  You have gone before us.  Thank you, Lord, for Your protection so far this day.  Please protect us as we are here and as we travel home.  Love you, Lord.*

He was around the truck, helping Raleigh out and then reaching for the flowers that he had insisted that he needed to bring to her mother.  She had told him that wasn't necessary, that her mother would not expect that.  He had simply kissed her cheek, startling her.

Rori had been seated on the front steps, anxiously waiting for Raleigh.  She was in danger, he knew, and he wanted to take that from her.  Only, it wasn't his place.  Not any more.  And that would take some adjusting to step back.  He simply wrapped his twin in his arms and held on tight.  He felt her sobs as she tried to control them but couldn't quite.

Richard watched, compassion on his face for the siblings.  He was aware of how close they were. Raleigh had talked about her family, just to prepare him, she said.  He looked up as the door opened and her parents emerged.  Ross stood at the top of the stairs, assessing Richard before he walked down to shake his hand.  He had had a talk with Abe the night before and had welcomed his assessment of Richard.

"Welcome, Richard, to the family.  We can't tell you how welcome you are and how grateful we are for the step that you took."  Ross wiped at his eyes, unable to control his emotions as his daughter stepped into his father hug.

Rebekah reached to hug Richard before she too turned to her daughter.  Richard watched as the two ladies sobbed before Ross moved them towards the house.  He stood for a moment, feeling the eyes watching them.  They had been followed, he knew. Richard had been aware of a truck hanging far enough back from them that he could not get a good description of it.

Rori watched his brother-in-law closely, not sure what to expect from him. He knew of his occupation, also having had a talk with Murphy, one of Abe's team members and his partner as well. He had been impressed, to say the least.

"Richard? You're troubled." Rori pointed towards the house.

"I am. I think that we brought trouble to your home." Richard stepped inside the doorway and removed his shoes, an automatic habit for him.

"More than likely. We'll deal with it. Frankie has been around and spoken with us, given what you two are facing. What can I do to help?"

"At the moment, I am not sure. You are praying for us. That helps. Raleigh is in danger. We just don't know from whom or why."

"But so are you." Ross had approached the two younger men. "Come, Richard, we're in the living room. This is now your home."

Richard nodded, walking that way, finding Raleigh on her feet, reaching for him. Her family saw that and wondered. Raleigh had always been independent, insisting that she could stand on her own feet.

Ross and Rebekah shared a look and then a nod. God had provided just the man who would reach down into their daughter's heart, to the hidden depths that she very seldom showed any of them to others.

---

# Chapter 17

Heading home late that evening, Richard yawned. The stress had taken its toll on his body, still healing from the accident and the beating. He had been welcomed into Raleigh's family, and made to feel a part of the family. Rori had taken him to one side before they left, asking what he could to help. As an artist who did glass blowing art, Rori wasn't sure that he even could.

"Watch your back, Rori. If they can't get to Raleigh, they may come after you. Be aware at all of times who is around you. Talk to Abe or Frankie. They'll be able to give you advice on that. Watch out for your parents too."

"I will. Dad's in his studio all day but he does travel back and forth. Mom's a teacher. She's talked to the school, and they're aware that she may be a target."

"Thanks for that, Rori. Listen, if you want to head my way anytime, you're welcome. It's Raleigh's home now."

"Thanks, Richard. We appreciate it. All we ask is that you take care of her and of yourself. It's a puzzle as to why."

"It is. We're working on it. Bill is working the investigation although he doesn't have a lot of information at the moment. That means our investigation gets shifted to the side. Not what we want but it's how life works."

—

Raleigh was content.  Richard had been welcomed by her family, drawn into their circle.  Her father had approached her before she left, hugging her. He told her that he was impressed with her husband, that his faith shone through in every word that he said. She had hugged Ross back, thanked him, and then walked to where Richard was waiting for her.

"Happy, love?" Richard's voice broke through the dimness in the cab.

"I am.  Thank you, Richard, for today."  Her head turned on the headrest as she studied what she could of him in the dim light.  "You were welcomed into the family."

"I was.  Just as you were into mine."  Richard drove in silence for a while.  "What about your cabin? Do you need to retrieve anything from there?"

Raleigh shook her head.  It was no longer her home.  Richard's house had become that.

"No, I don't think so.  I don't want to sell it." That thought saddened her.

"We won't.  We'll use it as a retreat or second home.  I like it.  I would like to see it when I can actually take in what is there."  He grinned as she snorted.  "Really, I do.  I don't remember much about it."

"No, you wouldn't.  Now, about tomorrow?  All of your team is coming?"

"They are.  And their spouses."  Richard paused, not sure how to express himself.  "I'm glad that you're mine, Raleigh.  I have wanted someone of my own for

———

years. I just had to wait for God. With the others marrying, it felt odd to be the only one without someone. Thank you for being who you are." He didn't expect Raleigh to answer, not realizing that he had put his heart out for her to see.

Raleigh couldn't speak. Her emotions overwhelmed her for a moment. She simply rested her hand on his wrist and squeezed.

The next morning, Raleigh stood inside the church door, almost afraid to walk forward. Richard had her hand in his, waiting for her to move. For however long it took, he would wait. If it meant that they turned around and walked out, then they would.

Raleigh looked up at him, seeing his confidence in her decision. His look signalled that he backed her fully.

"Where do you usually sit?" Raleigh walked towards the doors to the sanctuary, not seeing the eyes on her and Richard and the surprise on the faces around them.

"At the back. I sometimes have to leave and I find that the best." Richard seated her, nodding at his friends before he sat beside her, reaching for her hand. "It's okay, love. You're part of our family here."

"I was, but not like this. This has changed." Raleigh shifted closer to him without knowing that she had. "Someone's in here, Richard. I can feel them."

"I know. So can I. My team will seat around us. Bill and Cora are moving in beside you. We have put out word to the officers and church officials about what

is going on.  We will be as safe as we can be here."
Richard was on guard.  He had strapped on his weapon
that morning, unbeknownst to Raleigh.  He knew that
his team members were also armed.

That afternoon, Raleigh paused as she stepped
out onto the back porch.  The four other couples had
just moved in on her, the ladies drawing her aside.  She
had enjoyed the time with them, finding that she was
not judged.  She had expected that.  Raleigh had also
heard their stories, shock on her face as she listened.
Her thought was that she had someone here in town
who she could speak with.  That helped relieve some
of her stress.  She knew from them that others of their
friends had faced the same.  Raleigh had not known
that their pastoral couple, Silas and Madigan, and Bill
and Cora had faced danger as well.

Richard came looking for her.  He had had to
answer a call from the head of the team due in the next
day.  That had disturbed him.  He had wanted to just
spend the day with Raleigh.  That had not happened.

"I'm sorry, love.  That sometimes happens."
Richard wrapped an arm around her, just standing with
his eyes on her.

"It's okay, Richard.  I understand.  It's your job
and who you are.  You can sometimes expect that with
me.  I'll get called in on short notice sometimes.  That's
life."

"It is.  It doesn't make it any easier."  Richard
turned her to the swing on the back porch, drawing her
down onto it and starting it into motion.  "This is a
favourite time on a Sunday for me.  Late afternoon.  I

—

get to relax and rest, spend time communing with my Lord.”

“It’s the quiet time before the busyness of the week starts.  I agree with you.”  Raleigh grew pensive.  “Where does the investigation stand, Richard?”

“I don’t know.  I didn’t get a chance to speak with Bill this morning.  I suspect that they’ve had to set it to one side.  We don’t have enough information to move forward.”

“Kat called me when you were outside.  She’s working through our family trees and will forward them to us.  She wants us to go over them very carefully.  And Emma is back from wherever it was that she had had to travel to.  She’s starting her searches, she said.”

“And she will find something.”  Richard too grew pensive, his thoughts muddled, a rarity for him.

# Chapter 18

Two days later, Raleigh ran for her office building, fear leading wings to her feet. She heard the car pulling in behind her and running footsteps pounding on the pavement behind her. She frantically punched in her security code, yanked open the door, and pulled it tightly closed behind her. Raleigh leant back against the door. The door jerked against her back as heavy fists pounded at it. Her phone was out in a moment as she called for help.

Finally able to make her feet work, Raleigh headed for her office, dropping her purse into a drawer and then sitting. Her head was buried in her hands.

Hearing the front bell ringing, Raleigh jumped and then was on her feet. Walking slowly towards the door, she peeked out, relieved to see patrol officers there. She reached to unlock the door.

"Mrs. Ransome? Are you okay?" The first officer stepped into the waiting room, watching as Raleigh wrapped her arms around herself.

"I don't know. Who were they?" Raleigh shuddered at how close it had been.

"They didn't mean you any good." The officer took her statement before he stepped outside once more.

Raleigh paced. She was the only one in the office at the moment, coming in for an early shift. She had needed to be in the office that day. She was regretting that now. Richard would never let her drive

—

in on her own again, she decided, knowing that she would need to call him. That was a call that she didn't want to make.

Bill approached Raleigh about an hour later. He had been paged as he had driven in to work, detouring so that he could speak with her.

"Raleigh?" He waited until her head was raised from her work. "May I?" He pointed to a chair in her office.

"Sure. Why not? It's not like I'm really getting much done." She frowned at his grin. "What can you tell me?"

"The men were still here when the officers arrived. We have been able to arrest them. Not that they're talking."

"No, they never do. I don't understand, Bill. Why me? Why Richard? We're from different towns. How are we connected? We've tried to figure it out without any success."

"We're not much further ahead. Emma has sent some information that she's found. She's sending it to you and Richard as well. It's puzzling, Raleigh. It could be related to your personal lives. It could be related to your professional lives. That's a hard one to determine."

"I know that it is. We've been working on it at home, as you say. So has his team. We're just not getting anywhere. And we should."

"Yes, we should. We're missing something. And just what that it? We don't know. I need to sit down with you and Richard again." Bill walk away after more questions, some of which Raleigh was not able to answer.

Richard rose to his feet as he heard Bill's voice speaking with Stephen. He walked to his office door, finding Bill watching him.

"Bill? I don't like it that you're here." Richard pointed to the chair in front of his desk.

"I don't like it either. Have you heard from Raleigh today?"

"Not since she left for work." Richard's face turned stern. "What has she not called me about?"

"She was followed this morning. She was just able to get inside her work building. Patrol did arrest the men who are not talking." Bill handed over his phone with the photos of the men pulled up. "Do you recognize them?"

Richard's face grew sterner.

"I do. They were there that day. The one on the left? He's the one who held the gun on Raleigh. The other stood at her other side. Who are they?"

"We don't have any identification on them as yet. With your identification today, then we can hold them for that as well as today. I just don't know how long that they will be in jail for."

"That's the worry." Richard looked around, on his feet as Raleigh appeared, Stephen and Timothy behind her, worried looks on their faces. "Raleigh?"

Raleigh simply threw herself at him, finding his arms closing around her and making her feel so safe and yes, she thought, cherished.  She had had a long talk with her supervisor.  For now, she was on leave until this was settled.  A decision on whether or if she returned to her work would be made at some point in the future.  She just could not put her fellow employees or clients at risk.  Her thought at the time had been to find Richard and ask if that was what the man wanted, for her to leave her work.

Richard reached for her and drew her into his office.  He shoved her into a chair, crouching beside her, an arm wrapped around her. She was shaking with fear and couldn't frame a word.  He took with thanks the opened bottle of water that Silver handed him and made her sip at it.  Richard could hear conversation behind him but his full focus was on Raleigh.  He knew that his team would be alert, searching her vehicle, and then spreading out to search the area.  The team that was training had been in the office and was quickly paired up with one of his team to search.  Life had just become real for them.

Bill sat back down, his note pad out ready to talk with Raleigh.  He shared a look with Richard, simply shaking his head.

"Bill, can you get Stephen?  I need him to assess her. If I need to take her in to Emergency, then I will."

Stephen, the team's paramedic, was back in no time, his kit in his hand.  He quietly and quickly assessed Raleigh, sitting back on his heels when he finished.

"She's in shock, Richard."

"That's what I thought. Do we need to take her in?" Richard was prepared to simply sweep her into his arms and head that way.

"No, I don't think so. Let me go make a call. I'll be right back." Stephen was away, calling a good friend who worked in the Emergency Room as a physician. He agreed to head their way, just finishing his shift. Stephen was back beside Raleigh, reaching for her wrist to take her vitals once more. "James is on his way. He's just finished his shift."

"Thank you, Stephen." Richard did not move from beside Raleigh until James had arrived. He rose and stepped back into the hallway, leaving Stephen and James in the office. Bill touched his arm.

"Has this happened before, do you know?" Bill's voice was quiet

"Not that I am aware of." Richard scrubbed at his face. He knew that his team was still there, not willing to leave until they knew that Raleigh was fine. "I don't know. I would have to ask her parents. And I'm not doing that until I know that Raleigh is alert and able to answer any of our questions." He turned back to the doorway, listening to the quiet conversation between the two men in the office. He saw the moment that Raleigh looked up and looked for him. He was beside her on his knees, finding her wrapping her arms around him.

"Do we need to take her in, James?" Richard didn't look up. His whole attention was centre on Raleigh.

———

"No, not at the moment. She's coming out of her shock.  What caused it?"

"She was followed and then chased into her work.  From what Bill said, she barely made it inside."

James searched the faces gathered around Raleigh and nodded.  He didn't need to be told that Richard and Raleigh were in difficulty.  He could only pray that they escape relatives unscathed.

# Chapter 19

Raleigh looked up that evening to find Richard watching her before he approached and sat beside her. He simply wrapped her in his arms, tucking the blanket closer around her. Her head went down on his shoulder. She was still cold and still feeling the effects of her shock.

"Getting better?" Richard's voice was low, concern evident in his tone.

"I think so. What happened?" Raleigh still had not talked about what she had gone through that morning.

"You went into shock. Somehow, you managed to drive yourself home. We think that as soon as you realized that you were safe, you shut down. Stephen looked you over and then had a friend, a physician, come in and assess you. Physically, you're fine. But we do need to talk about it."

"We do. Bill came to my office and talked to me."

"He was here when you got home. He came out to talk to me. Has this ever happened before?" Richard waited patiently, letting her have the time that she needed to process his request. All he could do was pray for her.

"I don't think so unless it was when I was tiny. Mom and Dad would know best." Raleigh yawned, fatigue hitting her hard. "Can I sleep, Richard?"

He smiled at her request, knowing that she had already slipped away on him. He simply sat, holding the love of his life, his heart heavy for her. Richard wanted the men responsible for terrifying her. He just didn't know how to find them. This was not the way it was supposed to be.

The next morning, Raleigh was on her feet, surprised to find herself still in the living room and in Richard's arms. She smiled a somewhat sad smile, knowing that he had not moved that night. Instead, he had held her just for her to feel safe. Raleigh dropped a kiss on his cheek before she headed for her bedroom, intent on a shower and clean clothes. A tap at the front door detoured her that way.

Bill stood there, a stern look on his face. He sighed to himself. Raleigh looked rough, he noted.

"Bill? You're here early. If you want, head for the kitchen and start coffee. Richard's still asleep in the living room." Raleigh hesitated until Bill smiled at her.

"Go and do what you need to, Raleigh. I'll start your coffee and wake Richard. He needs to be present when we talk."

Raleigh nodded before she climbed the stairs and headed for her bedroom. She grabbed clean clothes and headed for the shower. She stared in shock at her face. Dark circles were under her eyes. There was a strained look on her face, one that was not normal for her. She dressed quickly and headed for the stairs.

Bill turned as he heard shuffling footsteps approaching. Richard appeared, nodding at Bill before he squinted at the clock. It was way too early for him to be there, but there had to be a reason.

"Bill? You're here? And you're early?" Richard turned as he heard Raleigh approaching him. "Raleigh? I didn't hear you leave."

"No, you were sleeping." She moved to hug him before passing him and heading to pour herself a mug of coffee. "Bill? You're too early to be here. What's wrong?"

Bill grinned at her, knowing what she was up to. Richard pulled out a chair and made Raleigh sit, setting her mug in front of her. He reached for the loaf of bread even as Bill reached for eggs from the fridge. This was not the first time that they had prepared a meal together.

"Nothing is really wrong, Raleigh. I was back around your work earlier. There are signs that intruders have been around. Our patrol vehicles were around at the time. The officers have arrested more men."

"They're not giving up, are they? I just don't know what they want." Raleigh became lost in thought, not seeing the glances that both men were throwing her way.

"Raleigh? Have you remembered anything that will help?" Bill sipped at his coffee, his eyes on Raleigh.

Raleigh shook her head, a frown momentarily appearing on her face.

"No, I don't think so. I'm not sure about what happened yesterday. I didn't see the men. I just ran."

"And it's good that you did. It's not likely that you would be here today if you hadn't." Bill was afraid for his friend and his lady. There was something that they need to find and couldn't to solve the investigation. "I will need to speak with your family at some point."

Raleigh stared at him and then down. Richard wrapped an arm around her, his prayer whispering in her ear.

"They expect that. I understand that you know Frankie."

"I do. I have spoken with him. We'll continue to do that. We want this over for you, Raleigh. You feel that you can't go on with your life until it is. And you also feel that you are bringing danger to Richard and his team and their spouses."

"I am. I just don't know why." Raleigh leaned her elbows on the table, her face thoughtful. "I have gone back over everything that I can to when I was young. I can't remember anything unless there is a family that resented their family member being in hospice care. I not likely would have been told. You'll need to speak with my supervisor."

"And we're working on th warrants for that. She's agreed to speak with us once we have that in place. Richard?"

Richard shook his head. He was at a loss as well.

"I'm sorry, Bill.  I just don't know.  It's like someone is placing cat and mouse with us.  We're the mice.  I can't say as I like that all too much."

"None of us did, Richard.  And you know what Cora and I went through.  Andrew and Phoebe as well."  Bill paused speaking, his eyes on Raleigh.  "I think that we three couples need to meet and discuss what we went through."

"I agree.  I think that would be a good idea for Raleigh to hear your stories.  She's heard my team's.  She's heard her friends in Riverville.  We're planning on getting together with Josiah and that group of friends on the weekend."

"Just so Raleigh isn't overwhelmed."  Bill was watching Raleigh, seeing her nod at his comment.  He sighed once more to himself.  This was not how the day was to go, he decided.

# Chapter 20

Richard walked through the downtown area the next day, his thoughts troubled. He had no idea of what to do or where to go. And that was unusual for him. This time, it was different. This time, it affected him and the lady who he finally acknowledged that he loved. He headed for Ev's diner, hoping to find Avery there.

Ev watched him sit at a booth before she reached for two mugs of coffee and sat across from him, their coffees in front of them. She had no idea why they always had to have a mug of coffee to talk, but that was how it was.

"You're troubled, Richard." Ev looked up as she felt someone beside her and moved over to let Andrew sit.

"I am, Ev. Andrew, I didn't see you." Richard rubbed at his cheek. "This is not making sense. Bill was around. He said there is one piece of evidence that they need."

"It's true, Richard." Andrew spoke up. "It's always that way. And it is usually something that is in plain sight that trips us up."

"It is. We're working it just as we did for the others. It's not making sense." Richard was puzzled at that.

"We know that you would be. I hear that Emma has been in touch."

"She has been." Richard slid over on the seat to let Avery sit beside him. "Avery? Have you heard anything?"

"Not a word. And given your line of work, I should. That tells me that someone is watching you very closely. Someone in town is involved." Avery rose for a moment and then returned with their meals.

"I agree with that assessment." Andrew asked the blessing on their meal before he studied his friend. "How is Raleigh?"

"She's hurting, Andrew. She's afraid and not sure how to react or who to trust outside of my team and our friends. She's not working at the moment."

"It's probably better that she's not. What can we do for her?" Andrew was thinking fast, trying to come up with something that would help move the investigation along.

"For now? Pray for her. We need to put her in touch with the ladies who can meet with her and pray with her. She's been isolated since she moved here." Richard felt bad about that even though there was nothing he could have done about it.

"She's been watched for a while, I would suspect." Avery shared a look with Andrew. "I'm still putting out feelers, Richard. Not that anything has come back. It's strange that there hasn't been."

"That's what I don't understand. It's unusual to have that happen. Ev? Have you heard any rumours?" Richard turned to her, watching the emotions that flickered across her face.

"No. Not that I know of. I'll ask the staff if they have heard anything." She moved away from them, Avery with her.

"Andrew? What are your thoughts, now that we're on our own?" Richard reached out to his friend, knowing that Andrew would be honest with him.

"My thoughts? That this is far from over. I can't tell you how to protect yourself. You're well aware of what needs to be done and what to watch for. As to how we solve this? Bill's working it as he can. So far, we don't have enough information that we need. And you're not getting the parcels and the letters and the voicemails that normally come. That tells me that they are close to you and watching both of you very carefully."

"That's what our consensus is. We're followed when we're out. Someone is around the property, not close enough to catch any information on them." Richard played with his fork, turning it over and over. "Raleigh is spooked. I don't know how to help her."

"And you will. Just be there for her. Be with her when she's out and about. It's hard, given how you married. But you're married and I know you won't walk away from her ever." Andrew watched his friend. "That's how I was about Phoebe."

Richard once more walked along the main street of his town. He stopped for a moment, a thought running through his mind. He spun on his heel, heading back for a store, ducking inside, making his purchases, and then running for his truck. He needed to find Raleigh.

Raleigh stared at Richard in horror before she was tugging at the ring on her finger.  It popped off before she dropped it on to the table.

"You think something is in them?"

"It is entirely possible, Raleigh. That may be how they are monitoring our activities."  He reached for the bag that he had dropped onto the table and dumped it out.  His hand reached for hers as he opened one of the boxes.  His fingers held the red-gold engraved wedding band.  He slipped it on her finger, before he slid the one off of his own.  He handed her his matching band, waiting for her to study it, study him, and then study his finger before she slid it on.

Raleigh stepped into his hug, feeling better about the rings.  She had studied hers many times, wondering why they had to wear those rings.  She now studied Richard, finding him reaching for another box.

"I know that we married under duress, Raleigh. I just wanted you to know that I would still have chosen you."  He held up a beautiful emerald ring.  "Would you accept this as my commitment to you?"  Richard waited for her to speak or nod or shake her head.

Raleigh blinked, surprised at his words.  She silently held out her hand, not sure what to say.

Richard hugged her, feeling better with the new rings. He dumped the discarded rings into a bag, determined to get them to Bill as soon as he could.

"We'll get there, love." Richard leaned down and kissed her forehead before he walked away, the bag with the rings tucked into his pocket.

Raleigh stood with a hand over her mouth. She had not expected the kiss but still welcomed it. Richard was working his way into her heart more and more each day.

Stephen sat back from his computer monitor, a frown on his face. He had received an email on his work account about Richard and Raleigh. He didn't know who the author of the email was. He printed it out before he saved it and then forwarded it to his team members and then to Bill. On his feet, he headed for Naomi.

"Naomi? I just sent you a copy of this email. I don't get it." He handed over the printed copy of it.

"An email? About Richard and Raleigh?" Naomi took it and read through it. "This doesn't make any sense, does it?"

"Not at all. I wish that Richard was here to speak with but he's at the meeting out of town. Raleigh's off site as well."

"She is? I didn't know that." Naomi started her search before she turned. "Where is she?"

"With Phoebe, Cora, and Madigan. I think some of the other ladies were to be there. Richard arranged it so that Raleigh could hear their stories. He's worried that she feels isolated."

"And she has been. He's right on that." Naomi turned back to her computer as she heard a chime. "What's this?" She pointed to the screen.

Stephen read the article before he asked for a copy and then the link to be sent to him.

"We need to meet as a team, Naomi, even without Richard. It's time that we're starting to make plans."

"I know. Silver's due back about now. She'll work this more thoroughly than I can. I'll find some houses that we can use. We may need to head for Riverville."

"We may. I reached out to Abe. He's adamant that he wants to be involved. And Don is back next week. He'll be around to find out what's going on. He's been worried about Richard." Stephen walked away, heading outside to find Timothy.

Abe turned from staring out of his living room window, finding Emma heading for him, a sheaf of papers in her hands.

"Abe? Do you know where Richard is today?"

"Not offhand. He did say something about a meeting out of town. In Oak City. Why?"

"This!" Emma shook the papers. "There's a hit out on him, intended for today. We need to reach him."

Abe grew grave, his phone out to call Richard. Only getting voice mail, he reached out instead to the police chief of that town, a friend of longstanding. He arranged for officers to find Richard and then escort him home. He knew that Emma would have reached out to Bill or Andrew.

Raleigh was shaken by the ladies' stories. Even though she had been told that they had had adventures, she had not expected to hear of what they had actually gone through.

"I didn't know it was like this." Raleigh sat back in her chair, a hand rubbing at her cheek. "How did you ever do it?"

"God. He's the first One that we turned to. And then each other. Our guys provided the support that we needed just as we supported them. We had friends to help as well. And Richard and his team were there for us. And so were Don and his team. Emma helped as well, finding the information that helped bring the culprits to justice." Phoebe leaned forward, intent on Raleigh. Her little daughter was cuddled in her arms. "You are not alone, Raleigh. Never that."

"No, you're not." Cora spoke up. "It may feel as if you are but you're not. I can guarantee you that you will be tired of seeing us. We walk in and out of each other's lives all the time. We have to support one another. That's what we do as sisters in Christ."

Raleigh nodded, rising to her feet at last. She had a lot to think about and a lot to discuss with Richard. Surprised to find Stephen waiting for her, she frowned at him.

"Stephen?" She sighed. "Now what?"

"Now what is that I drive you home. Timothy follows us. Abe called. There has been a hit put out on Richard. We need to keep you as safe as we can."

"Thank you, Stephen. I know that you will try. It's up to God if that works or not." Raleigh seated herself in her car, watching as Stephen drove away. "I guess changing the rings set off something."

"Rings? What are you talking about?" Stephen was confused.

"Our rings. Richard had us change them yesterday. He was taking the original ones to Bill this morning. Did our changing them set them off?"

"It might have. I'll have to speak with Emma again to find out more information. For now, until Richard gets home, we're with you."

"But you have plans for tonight. You must do." Raleigh was upset at that.

"No, we don't. We need to do this for you. Abe was reaching out to the police department in Oak City and arranging for an escort for him. What time was he due home?" Stephen pulled up to the garage and parked. His hand rested on her arm. "Wait until we know it's safe. Timothy, Naomi, and Silver are around here. One of them will come and find us. If we wait in the car, then we can take off if we need to."

Raleigh nodded, knowing that Stephen was right. She waited, somewhat impatiently, for word to come that it was safe for her to run to her home.

Richard thanked the officers who had escorted them before he paused as he walked towards the house. He watched as three of his team searched around his house. He then saw Raleigh and Stephen waiting in her car. He walked that way, Stephen stepping from the car.

"Stephen?"

"You're home. Good. We're just clearing the area before letting Raleigh go into the house."

"I am.  Abe reached out to you as well?"

"He did."  Stephen walked Richard around the car before Richard helped Raleigh out and walked her to the house.

# Chapter 22

Raleigh headed for the office building in the morning. She was worried, more worried than she had been. She paused for a moment, staring at the papers she held in her hand. Absorbed in what she was reading, she didn't hear the running footsteps until arms swept around her and just picked her up and ran away with her. A gag was slapped across her mouth before she could give more than one scream. Shoved into a vehicle, Raleigh began to fight, struggling to free herself from the hands that held her. A prick on the arm startled her before her fight to escape slowed and she dropped unconscious.

Richard looked around a couple of hours later. He thought that Raleigh was in the building and she wasn't. He was on his feet, out of the office door, and running for the house. He slid to a halt as he saw the scattered papers. He reached for them and stopped, stepping backwards.

Naomi had appeared, watching as Richard had stopped.

"Richard?" Naomi's voice reached through the fog that he seemed to be in.

"Call for help, Naomi. Raleigh's disappeared. I'm heading to search the house." Richard was off on a run, leaving Naomi heading for the office building and calling for the others.

Stephen turned from Naomi, moving rapidly to where they kept the feed for their security system. He worked backwards, stopping as he saw Raleigh taken. He sighed to himself before making a copy of it. Bill would want that.

Bill and Lily, another detective on the force and a good friend to the ladies on the team, searched along with the patrol officers that had responded. Stephen and Timothy stood on either side of Richard, flanked by the two ladies. Richard was more worried than he would admit, his arms folded across his chest. All he knew was that Raleigh had disappeared and from their own property.

Bill walked slowly towards the house as dusk dropped. They had spent hours searching for Raleigh, even to calling in the K9's. Her scent stopped where the papers had fallen. They knew that meant that she was carried away and that meant she had not gone on her own.

Lily hesitated before she spoke, not sure how to phrase what she wanted to say.

"Bill? What do we actually know about what is happening?"

"Not a lot, Lily. I spoke with Andrew a while ago. He wants you to concentrate on this for now unless you need to work on another case. You knew the routine only too well." Bill looked up at the darkening sky. "I have no idea where she is. None of us do. And that bothers us greatly."

Lily nodded, having gone through this too many times.

"I'll talk with Jason Long as well. He knows Richard well. They grew up together as well. Don is another one I'll reach out to." She blew out a breath. "It could go back to one of his assignments."

"Or it could go to one of Raleigh's clients. Or it could not be related to either one of those situations. We just don't know."

"I know. Emma's called me. She heard somehow what had happened. She said that Kat was working on family trees for both Richard and Raleigh and was sending them to Richard. I'll ask if I can have a copy to work from. Darci's in touch as well. She has a profile that she's working on." Lily stepped into Richard's kitchen, not seeing him but knowing that he was around somewhere.

"Where's Richard?" Bill walked through the kitchen, searching for him. "Richard? Any word?"

"Not a word. Any sign outside?" Richard didn't think that there would be but he still had to ask. His hands ran through his hair for the umpteenth time.

"Nothing. I'm sorry. Raleigh seems to have disappeared from where we found the papers. We have looked at them. Lily has them and will return them to you. We don't know that they are related to her abduction." Bill sat in one of the upholstered chairs, watching his friend closely

Richard sat as well, defeat in his demeanour. He just wanted Raleigh there. Only she was somewhere else where they had no idea where she was or who held her.

Bill studied the living room, seeing subtle changes that Raleigh had made. He nodded. She was making it her home. He was glad to see that. He decided that Richard and Raleigh were well suited to one another.

"Walk me through what you two have found." Bill pulled out his note pad and pen.

"What we've found? To tell you the truth, Bill, we have not found anything concrete. We have the papers on the wall that you can take a look at. My team has worked on that as has Raleigh. We've talked to both our families. She's talked with her supervisor. We've talked to her friends in Riverville. We just can't get a handle on it. Not like we should have. And before you ask, we haven't had the letters, parcels, and messages that normally come through. We're being followed. The team searches our vehicles twice a day."

"I thought that what you would say. We're at a dead end. That was, until now. Now this becomes more important to us. Lily is working on it for now. I'll keep a finger in but she's your go-to person."

"Thank you for what you have done, Bill. We both know how hard this is." Richard was on his feet, heading for the office and shutting the door, closing out everyone. He sat on the couch, his head bowed, worry and defeat in his bearing. All he could do was cry out to God for safety and protection for his lady. He had to be prepared for the worst but prayed for the best.

Bill had stood as Richard had walked away. He turned to Lily, finding her nearby.

———

"He's hurting, Lily. Stay here for the night. There will be patrol officers around. I'm sending in a team with a system to track any calls that come in. But if it comes in on his cell, as it likely will, I don't know that we can track it very well."

"We'll do our best, Bill. Richard has been there too many times for all of us. Andrew called when you were talking with Bill. He's authorizing overtime for now. He wants this over and Raleigh back home as soon as we can." She gave a brief smile. "Maybe Old George will come through again."

"I pray that he does. We need him to." Bill walked away, his heart heavy for his friend. He stood for a moment, his eyes on the lighted windows of the house before he headed for his car.

# Chapter 23

Three days had passed since Raleigh had been taken from her home property. Searches were ongoing but had been fruitless up to that point. There had been no sign of her and no contact from her abductors.

Richard could not sleep and barely ate. Riley had appeared, moving in with his brother for the time being. He forced hm to eat and to lie down whether or not he slept. Richard was grateful for that. Rori had shown up as well the day before, simply stating that he was there to help. Where did Richard want him? Richard had stared at him and then simply hugged his brother-in-law, barely able to contain his tears.

His team watched their boss closely, moving in to help where they could. They had taken over his portion of the training, working through it as best as they could. The trainees had been shocked to hear of Raleigh's disappearance and pledged to help find her.

Richard turned that day, hearing the doorbell. Walking that way, he opened the door, not surprised to find Abe and Emma there. Standing back, he pointed to the office. Emma had hugged him, barely able to contain her tears. Raleigh was a friend, and she had grown very much afraid for her.

Abe had prayed with Richard before they started their discussion. Emma had left what she could, Abe had given what information he could, and then they had left. Richard had stood in the driveway, watching them before his head turned. The two brothers stood beside him.

"Have you been back at the cabin?" Rori had to ask, not knowing if Richard had been or not."

"No, I haven't. I have been avoiding it. I guess that I need to." He reached for his keys, finding Rori holding up his own keys. "Thank you, Rori. I just need to lock up the house."

"Already done, bro." Riley grinned at his brother. "Head for Rori's truck. We'll head out there and see if anything is there."

Richard paced along the path to the cabin, feeling watched and knowing that someone was out there.

"Someone's here, fellows. Watch yourselves." Richard waited as Rori unlocked the cabin and then switched on the lights.

Richard stepped inside, not sure if they would find anything or not. The three men searched, not finding anything. Richard headed outside, walking around the cabin, his keen eyes alert to anything out of the ordinary. There was nothing there.

"Nothing? Where to now, Richard?" Rori was not sure what happened next.

"We go home. Rori, you're welcome to stay with me. Riley is. Maybe we can come up with something. It's time to think outside the box for finding Raleigh." Richard grew quiet as Rori drove back to his house. He had no words to say. He could not pray but knew that the Holy Spirit was praying for him.

Two days later, Old George stood with his eyes on a house close to Richard's. He had received word that Raleigh was held there. He had stood there for an hour, seeing traffic coming and going. At the moment, there was little activity around it. He crept forward and tried the door, finding it opening under his hand. He crept inside, searching and finding the locked door. He unlocked it, shoving it open and peeking inside.

Raleigh spun as she heard the door open and then the silence. She knew Old George well. She almost ran to him, reaching for his hand and letting him pull her from the room and from the house. They ran quickly across the lawn and disappeared between houses, heading for a hiding place that Old George had.

"Raleigh? You're okay?" Old George, an undercover officer, was worried about her.

"I'm fine. They didn't hurt me. Richard?"

"He's fine, Raleigh. Just worried about you. We'll get you back to him." Old George pulled out his hidden phone and made a call. "Lily will come for you. Now, what can I get for you?"

Lily reached for her phone, frowning at it for a moment. She had just come from an interview with Raleigh's supervisor. She had been given information that she needed to verify. A breath of relief came from her. Lily headed for her car and then to find Old George.

Raleigh watched from the shadows as Lily approached Old George. He simply pointed towards Raleigh who ran towards Lily and then was shoved into her car.

"You're okay, Raleigh?" Lily was torn between taking her home or to the hospital.

"I'm fine. Just angry. And I want to clean up. I feel so dirty." Raleigh's voice held the fatigue that she was feeling. "Richard is okay?"

"He is. Just very worried about you. You disappeared into thin air." Lily bit at her lip for a moment. "You had papers in your hand that day. What had you discovered?"

"A name, Lily. A name from my past. I was heading for Richard to see if he recognized it. I didn't make it."

"We know that, Raleigh. We asked him about that name. He recognized it. That man wanted to take over Richard's team and couldn't. Richard reported him for fraud, among other things, and he went to jail. He's still there as he was charged and convicted of murder."

"So, does that rule him out at all?" Raleigh was hopeful that it had.

"No, it doesn't. We need to investigate him further."

"Then, talk to my parents. He knew my great-uncle, the one who left me the cabin." Raleigh grew silent for a moment. "It seems to come back to the cabin. How valuable in the land?"

"I'm not sure that we know. I will investigate that as well." Lily pulled to a stop near Richard's garage. "Richard is training this morning. Come on. Let's get you cleaned up and ready to meet him."

The officers who had been assigned to wait for a ransom note had left.  They had all come to the conclusion that there would not be one.  Instead, Bill had asked for increased patrols in the area.

Lily turned from putting on the coffee and reached to make Raleigh some toast.  The water had stopped running and she heard footsteps slowly descending the stairs, knowing that Raleigh was on her way back down.

Richard stared at Lily for a moment as he entered his home, confused to find her inside when he knew that he had locked it up tight.  Hope grew on his face as Lily simply pointed towards the rest of the house. He was running that way, finding Raleigh waiting for him. He simply swept her into his arms, thanking God for His protection and for returning Raleigh to him.

# Chapter 24

Lily wiped at the tears on her face. This had gotten to her. Raleigh was becoming a friend, and she felt that enough was enough for her friends.

Richard stepped back, his hands reaching for Raleigh's. He studied her, seeing the stress on her face once more.

"Where were you?"

"Just down the road." Raleigh drew in a deep breath, naming the homeowner. "He's part of the church leadership, Richard. How do we do this?"

"Did he hurt you?" Richard could see no obvious signs of any harm.

"No, just kept me locked in a room. Old George found me." Her brow wrinkled for a moment. "I'm not sure how he did. He just showed up and released me. He hid me until Lily showed up."

"And Lily has taken your statement." He wrapped her into another hug. "Come to the kitchen. Lily's made coffee and some toast for you."

Raleigh sat, waiting for the questioning to begin. When it didn't, then she spoke.

"What happened here?"

"Not a lot. We searched for you. Both Riley and Rori showed up. They left this morning to go back to work. We'll need to call our families. I sent out a text to my team. They'll be round in the morning."

"But it's Saturday. They can't do that." Raleigh was horrified at the thought even though she knew that was exactly what the team would do.

"They can and will. They're working hard on this. And yes, they are stopping and going home, leaving it for the next day. But I can see that you have a thought."

"I do. It all seems to come back to my cabin and the forest. How valuable is it?" Raleigh shared a look with Lily. "We need to look into that."

"And I will ask Samuel to help. He does title searches and may be able to ascertain that. If not, we'll find someone who can tell us that."

Lily rose at last, heading back for the office. She dropped into a chair in Bill's office, waiting for him to return. He simply shot his head at her for a moment before he too sat, reaching for a pad of paper and pen.

"What happened, Lily?"

"Old George came through. He found Raleigh and got her to safety. She's home now. I have her statement, not that she could say much. Nothing was asked of her and she was told nothing. It's strange."

"It is, but we'll think it through. Now, where does it stand investigation wise?"

"Not where it should." Lily was frustrated. "Raleigh asked about her property. I'm looking into that too. There just seem to be so many strings and unrelated pieces. We need to find the right string and pull it to bring all the pieces into place."

———

Bill grinned at her words but he knew what she was saying.

"We'll find that. I'll talk with Andrew and see if he has any word on her property. Rawley Reade was well know here."

"What did he do?" Lily asked her question idly, not really expecting an answer.

"He was a historian of the town, publishing many books." Bill's voice died away. "There's an answer for you."

"I know. I'll add it to what I'm looking into." Lily was on her feet, pausing for a moment. "She's hurting in many ways. We need to end this for them."

"And we will. It just takes some time." Bill watched Lily walk away before he reached for his phone. He had too many investigations on the go to not make the calls that he needed to.

Richard's team gathered in the morning, free from training for the next week. Raleigh was there and had insisted that the spouses be there if they could. All had shown up. Richard hesitated for a moment before he asked for a time of prayer. He ended their time, his powerful prayer simply stating that he knew that God was in control, that God had a reason for what was happening, and that God would protect them all. He quoted the verses that he loved about protection and help, ending it with his usual "I love You".

Silver took a look at Raleigh and simply asked her to tell them what had happened to her. Raleigh complied, giving as many details as she could. When she named the man who had abducted her, there was silence before heads began to nod. No one was surprised at the name.

"How do we prove it now, team?" Richard was adamant that it be solved and solved as soon as they could.

"We're free next week. We'll spend our time working on this." Stephen nodded at the rest, who agreed.

"What do we know?" Silver spoke up, her brow furrowed as she thought through what she thought was what they knew.

"It's on the papers in the home office. We'll move them to here." Richard was on his feet, heading for the house, Timothy and Naomi with him.

Raleigh watched them move away before she was on her feet.

"The conference room?"

Silver and Stephen moved with her, knowing that was where Richard would want them to work.

"Now, we need to make some plans." Raleigh turned to the spouses. "What do we do? This is a team effort. We need to make plans as a team."

"And we will." Stephen's wife, Shanli, spoke up, reaching for a pad of paper and a pen. "Richard has us well trained. We'll note down everything that we know, everything that we think, everything that we want to find out, who we suspect, who we can clear. That's what we do."

———

They all grinned at the look on her face before Shanli grinned back at them. The conference room began to buzz with conversation and laughter.

Richard looked around as he heard the door to the reception area open. He walked that way, not surprised to see Bill, Frankie, and Abe.

"You're all here. Is there a problem?"

"Not a problem. We're here to see what you are up to. Sounds as if you have all hands on deck." Frankie grinned at him. "May we?"

"Sure. Head on back. They're in the conference room." Richard's hand came out to stop Bill. "Bill? Isn't Lily working on this?"

"She is. I'm not here as an investigator. I'm here as your friend. I'm not on the clock. Now, if you were to find out anything that we need to know, I'll just call Lily and ask her to stop by." He grinned at his friend.

"That works. Thanks, Bill." Richard headed back for the group, Bill on his heels.

# Chapter 25

Raleigh straightened up late that afternoon. It was just Richard and herself in the room, the others scattering to their homes, promising to be back in the morning. Frankie and Abe had left after a couple of hours, leaving a mass of information that Emma had sent. It still needed to be worked through but that would come.

Richard had raised his head as Raleigh stood before he was on his feet, her hand in his as he headed for home. The office building was locked and secured behind them. Raleigh was tired, more tired than she thought she could ever be.

"We'll eat, love, and then spend some time seeking those verses that we need." Richard had read her rightly.

"Thank you, Richard. We need to do that, I think. We're too much into this. It's all becoming too confusing. A night away from it works." Raleigh bit into her sandwich. Neither one of them had felt like much to eat.

Richard reached for his Bible. They had settled into their favourite spot on the couch, Raleigh wrapped tight to him. She felt safe and cherished and loved that night, knowing in herself that Richard had her love.

"What verses do we need to start looking at?" Raleigh really wasn't sure

"Those on protection and safety. God is protecting us, love, whether it seems like He is or not.

It's what He does.  He hides us in the hollow of His hand and covers us.  He provides the crevices in the rocks. He does not ever leave us or forsake us. He only wants the best for us at all times.  Sure, we go through difficulties and dangers. It's part of being human.  He doesn't keep that from us.  It is in those times that we learn to trust more and more.  He desires nothing but the best for us."

"I get that.  It's just hard going through it.  I see that with the clients at work. Not one of them has asked for that fatal disease or diagnosis to hit them.  Their families don't deserve it.  But it happens.  It can't always be cured, whatever it is."

"No, it can't.  When we went out on assignments, we never knew if that would be the last time that we did.  We didn't know if something would happen that would maim or kill us.  God protected us every time. We have that faith in Him because we've seen Him at work."

"We do. And we have."  Raleigh's head went down on his shoulder.  "We need to talk at some point, Richard, about what happens to us after this is over."

"And we will.  Right now, I can only say that I don't want you to leave me.  Ever.  I have found the one lady God planned for me."

Raleigh twisted to look at him, seeing him staring straight ahead.  There was a vulnerability about him that was unusual.

"Do you mean that, Richard?"  She waited for his nod.  "Then, I guess I must confess that I don't want to leave.  Not ever."

_______

Richard had been waiting for her to speak, not hardly daring to breathe. At her words, he simply hugged her tighter, his head on hers. They would talk, but first they needed to end what they were going through. Richard was deeply afraid of what lay ahead. He knew only too well that danger was waiting right at the corner for them, ready to pounce as a lion would pounce on its prey. He could only pray that they survived.

The next morning, Richard stood back from his door, finding Bill and Lily both standing there. He frowned at them.

"You're here too early. We're just getting up." Richard felt out of sorts and disgruntled that morning.

"We need to talk, Richard. Where's Raleigh?" Bill walked towards the kitchen, Lily following after giving Richard a shrug.

Raleigh had hesitated at the top of the stairs when she had heard the doorbell. She sighed. She really did not want to speak with either Bill or Lily that morning, but it seemed that she would have no choice.

Richard wrapped her into a hug as she walked towards him, a prayer uttered for her.

"Good morning, love. Bill and Lily are here."

"I know. Did they have to come so early?" Raleigh paced towards the kitchen, a frown on her face as the detectives turned to face her. "You're here too early. It had better be important."

"It is, Raleigh." Lily pointed at her. "We have arrested two of the men who we think kidnapped you. We need you to confirm that."

Raleigh shrugged, not really caring about that any more. She just wanted to get on with her life.

Bill watched her closely, seeing something different about Raleigh and Richard that morning.

"Take a look at these pictures, Raleigh. We are aware that it is early." Bill almost slapped the photos on the table.

Richard's arms came around Raleigh as he once more whispered a prayer in her ear. Raleigh leaned back against him, drawing from his strength. Her gaze drifted down to the men before she frowned.

"I've never seen these men, Bill, Lily. Not in my entire life. If they were there, then it was when I was locked up." Her eyes raised, seeing Bill and Lily nodding. "Is that true?"

"It is, Raleigh. They work for the man. One of them turned himself in and named the other man. We've been interviewing them for hours now. They have warned of a plot against you two."

Raleigh snorted, bringing a brief smile to Richard's face.

"That's not news, Bill. So what is news?"

Bill sighed. Raleigh was not making it easy for him. Lily shook her head at him before she approached Raleigh, drawing her to one side. Richard watched carefully, ready to move in and rescue her if he needed to.

"Raleigh? This is very serious. This plot? The man or woman in charge is getting desperate. He or she has gone to the streets, looking for people to help abduct you. They don't mean that for your health. We're working through the names but at the moment, we don't have confirmation on them. The house where you were held? It burned down last night. That destroyed any evidence that we were not able to get a warrant in time to retrieve."

Raleigh simply kept her eyes on Richard, fear moving through her. She turned and almost ran from them, her feet pounding on the stairs as she fled for her bedroom. She flung herself across the bed, praying for protection for Richard and his team and begging God to end their adventure that day. She couldn't do anything more to help.

# Chapter 26

Richard walked slowly towards the training building a couple of hours later. He had been deeply disturbed by what Bill and Lily had to say. The ones after Raleigh and himself were taking steps to hide. Burning down the house proved that. The arson inspector had talked with Bill and confirmed that it was indeed arson. How did he protect the love of his life? He had no idea. He just knew that he had to.

Stephen shared a look with Silver before moving to stand in Richard's way.

"Richard? There's been a development. You're troubled this morning." He refused to move out of the path.

"I am, Stephen. We'll talk this afternoon. I know that we're meeting tomorrow, all of us. But this needs to be said first." Richard moved around Stephen, leaving the other man staring after him.

"What happened overnight?" Naomi had approached, Timothy beside her.

"I have no idea. He just said that we'll talk this afternoon."

Timothy's thoughts turned to the news that he had watched early that morning.

"The house where Raleigh was kept? I think it's the arson fire from overnight."

Stephen nodded, his thoughts tumbling around in his mind for a moment.

"That would do it. Let's get through what we need to. Naomi? You're not training today?" Stephen waited for Naomi to speak.

"No, I'm not. Richard asked yesterday if I could be with Raleigh. That's where I'm heading." Naomi headed for the house, finding Raleigh waiting for her. "Raleigh? You're up early."

"Yeah, well, I am. Bill and Lily were here far too early." Raleigh's tone was disgruntled.

"They were? Then, they were up all night. We need to pray for them as well as you. Where's your prayer closet?" Naomi grinned at her.

"Prayer closet? I haven't heard that word in years. I would say Richard's office. Come on. We'll grab our coffee and head that way. Richard wants to meet with everyone this afternoon."

"That's what he said. I'm with you for the duration of the day." Naomi continued to grin at her as they moved to the office and found seats.

"You are? Thank you, Naomi. God has blessed Richard with a team that is so wonderful, kind, and compassionate. You are God's hands and feet on earth." Raleigh didn't see Naomi blink against sudden tears. She was instead concentrating on the pattern of the rug under her feet.

Milling around in the kitchen at lunchtime, the team tried to keep their spirits up, even though it was difficult. This was coming to crunch time, as they called it, and they were all deeply worried about Richard and Raleigh.

Richard watched his team, assessing them. The stress of what all five of them had gone through was concerning. He had made it a habit over the years to speak with each one individually and bring in what help was needed. Today? He knew that they all needed counselling. The four couples were involved in that. He would have to seek it for himself, then, and his lady.

"Richard? What can you tell us?" Timothy spoke for the group as they would their way to his office, plates of food in their hands.

Richard nodded, knowing that Timothy was concerned as was the rest of his team. He would speak but first they needed to eat and then spend time in prayer.

Richard reached for Raleigh as their prayer time finished, finding her shifting towards him. He hesitated to speak, not knowing how to exactly express himself. That was a rarity for him.

"Richard, Bill and Lily were here early, Raleigh said. What did they have to tell you?" Naomi set her plate aside once more, her eyes on her boss.

"They were here earlier. They had been on crime scenes all night. They did say that the house where Raleigh was kept was burnt down."

"On purpose." Stephen nodded, having expected something like that. "Do we know who owned it?"

"We do. Samuel came through with some information. He's still searching. But what he said is disturbing. The property has changed hands many

---

times over the years, which in itself is not unusual. It is who was the original owner that we need to be concerned about. The last owner was a relative of his.”

“And you know who that is?” Silver had done some of her own research on the property.

“We do.” Richard gave the names, watching each one of his team carefully. He knew that each one had had their own problems with the owner over the last few years.

“He’s the one who’s been after you, Richard, all this time. He went after us knowing that he would get to you through us. That’s what we’ve thought all along. Someone was after you.”

“It has been our thoughts. This confirms it. Raleigh, we’ve told you what the team went through. I think that we also mentioned that with each one, something was left over as you could call it. That seemed to be directed towards me.”

Raleigh had spoken with Naomi at great length that day, trying to understand what all had happened. She had realized that there was something missing.

“I know that name, Richard. He’s caused problems for Mom and Dad in the past. He has relatives in Riverville.” Raleigh shifted her weight again, moving closer to him. His arm tightened around her.

“He does? We’ll let Lily reach out to Frankie. It’s better that it comes as an official request.” Richard was at a loss for a moment. “We’ll work on that tomorrow. If we need to make a trip back to Riverville, then we will."

Silver nodded, her phone in her hand.

"Emma's picked up on that name. She's sending it to us all. She said that she has not sent it to Bill or Lily as yet. She wants our input."

"Thank you, Silver. We'll look at it tomorrow. For now, head on out. You need the time with your family." Richard was on his feet, following his team, grateful for their confidence and trust in him.

Raleigh gathered the dishes, washed them, and generally set the kitchen to rights. She was puzzled about the person named. She was determined to speak with her parents and to do that as soon as she could.

Richard paused for a moment, watching her before he wrapped her in a hug.

"You need to talk with your people."

"I do. I'll call them this evening. What are you planning on doing right now?" Raleigh waited patiently, knowing that Richard would speak when he was ready.

"Right now? How be we spend some time in the Bible? We need all the promises that we can find." Richard turned her to the living room, seating her and then finding his Bible before he sat beside her.

# Chapter 27

The next morning, Raleigh stood back and just watched as the team milled around Richard's office. She sighed before she turned and walked away, heading for the sun room. She stood at the window, staring out, not sure where she needed or even wanted to be. Richard had followed her, not intruding but letting her have the space that she needed. He walked away at last, his heart breaking for her.

Stephen looked up from his laptop for a moment, a thought tugging at his mind. He turned to Silver, finding her frowning at her own laptop.

"Silver? There was a client a year or so ago that we had such a bad feeling about. Do you remember him?" Stephen could hear the silence in the room as he asked his question.

"I do. He fought us the whole time. Mike Severenson. He's related to the town accountant." Silver looked up, a frown on her own face. "He didn't like us. Didn't he threaten us?"

"He did. And we reported him to the authorities there in Oak City. I need to find that detective again."

"Here's his name." Naomi handed the slip of paper over to him. "He has family in Riverville from what I can remember him saying."

Richard's own head raised as he listened. He remembered that man only too well. The threats and implied threats had been brutal. If he could have pulled his team, he would have. He regretted it.

"Severenson? Him?" Richard reached for the paperwork that Silver had retrieved from the printer. "If I remember correctly, his family was deep into crime. We also suspected him of being involved. The way that we were asked to watch him for the courts was unusual."

"It was. I remember that we put in a lot of discussion on it." Timothy read through the paperwork. "Here. There's a link to Raleigh. His brother is high in Riverville politics." He looked around as he heard a sound.

Raleigh stood there, shock on her face. She knew Brice Severenson and had not realized that his family was into crime.

"Brice? I know him. He's involved?" She slipped into a chair, her legs shaking too much to hold her up. "And his mother died from a fatal disease. She lived here in town. It was before I came on staff. I can remember reading about her in the newspaper."

Richard's face grew even grimmer. They were finding information that they needed to verify and then pass on to Lily.

Silver was on her feet, taping up a new piece of paper on the wall, writing down the information as it was called out to her. Raleigh worked beside her, circling names and drawing lines between them. She stood back at last, a frown on her face.

"This is a mess." Raleigh rubbed at her face. "How do we set it out to make it clear?"

———

Timothy grinned at her as he rose and stood beside her, showing her his papers.

"This. I've been sorting it out as you two ladies have worked. See if it fits with what you've done." He handed her the paper and walked away, troubled at what they had found. Tate followed him, wrapping him in her arms.

Richard rose and came to stand beside Raleigh, an arm around her before he reached for the paper. He read it, fear growing in his heart for Raleigh and also for himself.

"Richard?" Raleigh's voice was soft, yet sounded so loud in his ears. "You're troubled."

"I am, love. I am. This is not what we need or want. This involved multiple towns and multiple police forces. This is growing day by day. We need to narrow it down. I'm just not sure that we can. Thoughts, anyone?"

Shanli had reached for the paper, reading it through before passing it on. Each one read it and made notes. They worked to combine what they had discovered. They just didn't know if they had been correct in their discoveries.

Richard locked the door late that night. Raleigh had retired, exhausted from the day. He was as well but he didn't feel that he could retire. He was expecting something to happen that night. He just had no idea what.

Walking through the house, Richard paused in his office, his eyes on the last paper that they had worked on. He knew that he had to pass it on to Lily. He had called her but she had not responded yet.

Yawning, Richard headed for the stairs. He paused at Raleigh's bedroom door before he tapped at it. Not receiving an answer, he opened it, the light from the hall streaming in and across the bed. He could hear the sobs that Raleigh was uttering in her sleep. He was across the room, on his knees beside her. His hug did little to comfort her. Instead, her sobs became heavier. Richard stood, lost in thought, before he laid down beside her and wrapped her tight to him. His prayer calmed the love of his life. Both slept, not knowing that the men were drawing closer to the house, not fearing being detected not the security system. The light from the moon moved gradually across the bed, Raleigh having left the drapes open.

Raleigh was on her feet in the early morning, turning to study Richard. She had been surprised to awaken, finding that she had not dreamt that night. Realizing that Richard had held her all night, she smiled slightly before she grabbed clean clothes and headed for the shower. It was Sunday and she was determined that they be in church. They needed it, she knew, afraid of what the coming week would bring.

# Chapter 28

The next morning, Raleigh headed for town. She had waved at Timothy as she drove away. She needed to get away and be by herself. Walking along the main street, Raleigh was lost in thought. She felt afraid but was determined not to give in to that for, not any more. She headed for the library, wanting to find some books to read. A thought distracted her and she turned, heading instead for a local music store. She browsed the music before she reached for a CD. This is the one, she decided, just what Richard would like.

Tucking it into her purse, Raleigh stood once more on the sidewalk, not sure where to head next. A voice speaking from beside her had her jumping. She turned. Madigan stood there along with Cora.

"Raleigh? You look lost." Madigan grinned at her. "We're heading to Ev's for lunch. We would like it if you would join us."

Raleigh hesitated and then nodded. She could do this, she decided. She felt peace about going for lunch with these new friends of hers.

Laughter filled their booth as they shared experiences from their youth. Raleigh studied the two ladies with her. She had needed this, she decided. She glanced at her watch. It was now mid-afternoon.

"I need to get home, ladies. I enjoyed this." Raleigh smiled as they agreed. "We need to do this again."

"And we will. We have a Bible study that meets on Thursday evenings. Join us when you feel safe enough to do so. The ladies are all Richard's friends."

"I will keep it in mind." Raleigh walked away, a small wave sent their way.

Old George was watching her, knowing that she had escaped for the day. He was very worried about her though. Word was reaching him on the street that the men after Richard and Raleigh were drawing in around them. He just didn't have the information or all of the information that he needed to go to Bill.

Driving home, Raleigh was not concentrating on the road or the traffic around her. She certainly didn't see the truck that was tailing her. She didn't see it accelerate towards her, striking the back of her car and sending it spinning across the road and into the trees. Her scream floated through the air before the car slammed into a tree. Her head hit the steering wheel. The eerie silence that followed echoed among the trees. It took many moments before the forest inhabitants began to creep cautiously out to stare at the large unmoving object.

Richard paced the driveway late that afternoon. Raleigh should have been back by now and wasn't. He ran for his truck, driving away and then searching along the road. He didn't see anything that alarmed him. Turning around, he drove back home, praying that Raleigh would be here. Only she wasn't. He could not put it off any longer. Richard reached for his phone, making the call that he dreaded, asking for help as Raleigh had disappeared.

Bill and Andrew walked towards Richard, watching him pace as the patrol officers searched around his house and buildings. They shared a look, knowing that Raleigh would not have walked away on her own.

"Richard? What can you tell us?" Bill's hand on Richard's arm stopped him.

"I don't know, Bill. She headed into town today, just needing some time by herself." He frowned at Bill. "She sent a text telling me that she was having lunch with Madigan and Cora."

"She did?" Bill had not been aware of that. "Do you know about what time she would have left to come home?"

Richard shrugged, reaching into the depths of what he could do and stiffening his spine. He needed to be strong for his lady. He just wanted to find her.

"I'm not sure. Cora or Madigan could probably tell you." Richard watched as Andrew stepped away to call one of them. "She's afraid, Bill. She knows Brice Severenson from Riverville. This is getting too bizarre. How do we do this?"

Bill shrugged, not sure what to say.

"I don't know, Richard. We have the information that Silver passed on to us. That's what you were working on Saturday. At least, I think that's what she said."

"It was. We had narrowed it down and tried to collate it as much as we can. Any of my team will speak with you about that."

"Lily's talking with them. She'll catch me up to date on that. Now, you say that you drove into town and back home?"

"I did. I didn't see anything. I don't know if she even left town." Richard paced in a circle, his hands jammed into his jacket pockets. "Where is she?" Richard began to pray, begging God to bring his lady home. He needed her in his life. He didn't know if he could go on if she didn't come back.

Andrew beckoned to Bill, drawing him away from Richard. A patrol officer stayed nearby, his eyes on Richard, ready to react if he needed to. This was done despite the fact that Richard was fully trained in security. This was different. He needed that protection himself this time.

Andrew pointed towards Bill's car, heading that way before he spoke.

"I called Madigan. They separated just after one. Madigan watched her drive away. Raleigh said that she was heading home. If that's the case, then she's somewhere along the road."

"That's what I'm afraid of, that's she's been run off the road. And in the dark, we'll never find her vehicle." Bill slapped at the roof of his car. "We need to search but I don't know that we'll have enough light to do that tonight."

"I think that you're correct. And if the temperature drops as it's supposed to, I'm worried about her." Andrew watched Richard closely. "He's right on the edge, Bill. He's trying to stay strong. It's hard when you're the leader and have to stay strong. He's been through so much with his team."

"He has been. I know that his team is supporting him but that doesn't help in this. They can only do so much." Bill headed back for Richard, a hand on his friend's shoulder to direct him back to the house."

# Chapter 29

Raleigh came back to her senses, or what she would consider her right senses. She shoved her hair from her face. Searching in the darkness, she frowned, bringing on a deeper headache. Turning off the ignition, she shoved at her door, just able to get it open. Raleigh stepped out, dropping to her knees as her head pounded with severe pain. She looked up, her eyes closing, feeling the cool night breeze on her face.

On her feet, Raleigh stumbled as she walked, her hands out to balance herself. She didn't know where she was. Then she decided that she didn't know how she was. Her stumbling steps took her forward, her hands reaching out to grab whatever it was that would help her stay on her feet. They ended up cut, scraped, and filthy.

She could never say afterwards how long she walked for. She just kept on her feet, moving in part to keep warm. Raleigh was searching for someone. She didn't know who and that person wasn't there.

Pausing at the top of a small grade, Raleigh stared at the cabin in front of her. It was dark with no lights. She drew sobbing breaths as she made her way down the small hill, falling numerous times and then crawling back to her feet. Her hands hit the cabin door as she hammered at it. There was no answer. Raleigh turned the knob, finding the door opening on creaky hinges. She stumbled inside, a shove of her hand shutting the door. She fell to the floor, unable to rise again. Her breath came in gasps before her vision faded and she was lost in that deep dark well.

A day went by. Then a second one passed. Raleigh had roused at times, crawling across the floor in a slow manner, reaching somewhere that she could find water. She sipped water as she was able to.

On the third day, Raleigh sat up, staring around at the cabin. She had no idea where she was. Raleigh rubbed at her face. She had no idea who she was either. Staring at her hand, she studied the rings. Raleigh decided that she was married. Was she on the run from an abusive husband? Or was it something else? Was she a widow even at her age?

Raleigh hauled herself to her feet, a hand out to balance herself as she did so. She searched for more water, finding some and uncapping the bottle. She prayed that whoever owned this cabin would be okay with her helping herself.

Finding a knapsack, Raleigh packed some of the bottled water and headed out of the cabin. She looked up at the sky, her eyes closing against the pain. She began to walk once more, her path staggering from side to side. She just kept putting one foot down ahead of the other, not knowing where she was heading or if she was heading towards help or away from it.

Raleigh came to another cabin as night drew close. She knocked at the door and then tried the knob, once more finding the door opening. She stepped inside, searching for the homeowner and not seeing anyone. Finding a blanket, she wrapped it around herself and laid down on the couch, asleep before she knew it.

The next day repeated itself. Raleigh just kept putting one foot in front of the other. Her head pounded with each step. She didn't hear the sounds of nature in her ears. On that afternoon, she reached a gravel road. Hesitating, she turned and walked in the same direction that she had been heading.

A car slowed as it approached her before it pulled ahead of her and stopped. The older woman stepped from it and laid a hand on Raleigh's arm, halting her steps.

"Are you lost, dear?" Her soft gentle voice roused Raleigh somewhat from her stupor.

"I don't know. I don't know where I am. Do you?" Raleigh walked around her to the passenger side door. "Are you giving me a lift? I would like that."

"I can, dear." The lady helped her into the car and then walked to slide behind the wheel. She didn't know where to take Raleigh other than to her home. Her husband, a physician, would be able to help her.

Pulling into the parking lot of a large building, the lady, Anna by name, hurried into the building, finding one of the men who lived there sitting in the foyer.

"Brady? I need your help. I found a young lady on the road. She's hurt and very confused. Can you come and help?" Anna was more worried than she wanted to admit.

"I can. Do you know her?" Brady, a paramedic, followed Anna to her car. He crouched down beside the open door, assessing Raleigh. He was surprised that she didn't react when he reached for her wrist to take her pulse. "Anna? Doc is home, I know. Can you find him? I'll take this lady to the infirmary."

"I can. Let me have your keys to unlock the door." Anna looked around as they walked towards the hallway leading that way. "Doc? You're here?"

"I am. Who do we have here?" Doc reached for his stethoscope as Brady laid Raleigh on the hospital bed.

"I don't know, Doc. Anna found her on the road, she said. She doesn't seem to have any identification with her."

"I see." Doc assessed her, stepping back. "I would say that she's been in an accident at some point in the last few days. I don't recognize her."

"I don't either. I'll put in a call to Dallas and see if he's heard of any missing persons." Dallas, a friend of theirs, was also a police detective.

"Do that, Brady. Head off now. I know that you and Fynn have plans for tonight."

Brady nodded, not walking away for a moment. *He was burdened for the young lady, around his age,* he thought. *Who is she, Lord? How can we help her? And where is her family?*

Anna reached for a warm, damp cloth to wipe at Raleigh's face and hands. She studied the young lady, wondering who she was.

# Chapter 30

Three days later, Richard walked the downtown area of Riverville, Riley and Rori on either side of him. The three men had searched daily for Raleigh, not finding her. That stressed them beyond what had ever stressed them before.

"Where is she?" Richard was losing hope, as much as he clung to it.

"I don't know, Richard. We're all searching. Coming here? She may have headed this way, seeking safety in her hometown." Riley was grasping at straws, he thought.

"None of our friends have seen her. And the streets are watching for her." Rori had searched the town over and over for her, even dragging in Abe and his team.

"I don't think that she's here." Richard turned and headed back for his truck. "She's not here. But where is she? Is she still even alive?"

"You have to trust that she is, Richard." Riley's hand stopped his brother's steps. "Did we search the area along the roads to your home?"

"They did some the first day." Richard turned to Riley, his eyes lighting up once more. "We didn't search off the road, did we?"

"No, we didn't. Come on. Let's do that." Rori was running for his truck, intent on following Richard back home.

Abe's team was waiting for Richard, to his surprise. His own team and their spouses were there. And Don and his team drove in after their vehicles.

"We're here to search, Richard. All of us." Abe stood, his arms crossed across his chest. "We pray first and then we search."

Hours passed as they searched. Murphy pointed at last to an area, heading that way with Don and Paul. They stopped abruptly, seeing the sunlight reflecting off metal.

"That's her car, Murphy." Don confirmed the license plate. Don's phone was out, calling it in to the police department. "We'll need to reach out to Richard but keep him away."

Murphy nodded, his eyes on the vehicles pulling to a stop at the side of the road.

"Richard's here." He walked towards Abe and Richard.

Richard's eyes were directed past Murphy to where Paul and Don stood. His head shook, before he heard Murphy speaking.

"Is she there, Murphy?" He was afraid to hear his answer.

"No, she's not. We haven't searched. We had just found it before you got here. The authorities are on the way."

"Thank you, Murphy." Richard's shoulders slumped as he turned and walked away, heading for where his team waited.

"What didn't you say, Murphy?" Abe knew his business partner only too well.

"There's not a lot of damage. She was run off the road by the looks of it, Abe. I have no idea where she could be. If she walked away, you would think that she would have headed for home."

Timothy had approached them, listening to their conversation.

"If she's disoriented from the crash, she may have headed away from the car, thinking to keep herself safe."

"That is what I think she did. I just pray that she found help somewhere." Murphy walked back to Don, his face stern with his thoughts.

"He's hurting, Abe. And we don't know how to help him."

"Just be there for him. Pray for him. Do what you can to search for Raleigh. I'm preaching to the choir here, Timothy, but you are well aware of what to do and what to look for."

Richard slumped in his chair that night, heartbroken at the thoughts of Raleigh out in the open for days. He couldn't pray at all. His heart prayed for him. He heard his parents talking in the kitchen and knew that Riley had seated himself near his brother, not saying a word.

Reynold walked towards his son, sitting nearby and praying for his son and his lady. He had put out feelers in the nearby towns, reaching out to friends who promised to reach out to their friends. They would find

Raleigh, he knew.  Just what condition would she be in when they did?  That was the question that no one wanted to answer.

Barnabas Carey approached Doc that night, concerned about the young lady who was now sleeping in Doc's spare room.  Anna had insisted on bringing her there.

"Doc, what do you know about her? Has she said anything?"

"Not a word."  Doc was puzzled as well.  "She's been awake but is sleeping now. When we asked her for her name, she didn't respond."

"I see.  Dallas will be around in the morning, he said.  What can we do to find out who she is?" Barnabas had seen his friends and employees of the Barnabas Foundation go through troubles as he had himself.  He didn't want to see anyone else do that.

"Good.  He can reach out to the neighbouring forces to see if there has been a report of a missing lady."  Doc was at a loss as was Barnabas.  "All we can do, Barnabas, is pray for her.  And that is the best thing that we can do."

"It is, Doc.  It is the most powerful tool that we have."

# Chapter 31

Raleigh shoved the blankets away from her the next morning, staggering to her feet and staring in panic. She had no idea where she was. A pile of clothing caught her eye before she reached for them. Searching the room and opening the doors, she found an ensuite and quickly cleaned up and dressed. Raleigh hesitated before she opened the door to the hallway, knowing that she would be questioned but not knowing the answers. She had no idea on how to answer.

Following the aroma of freshly-brewed coffee, Raleigh hesitated in the kitchen doorway. She didn't see anyone to ask if she could help herself to the coffee. Instead, she shrugged and did just that. A small sound behind her had her turning, fear on her face. The same lady stood there who had talked with her yesterday, she decided.

Anna smiled at her before she simply hugged her and then reached for bread.

"I'm Anna and you're in our home. Sit, dear, and I'll make you something to eat. You did tell us that you hadn't eaten for a few days."

Raleigh did just that, not knowing what else to do.

"I'm sorry. I'll leave when I eat. I just don't know where I belong. Do you?" Raleigh didn't look at Anna. She didn't want to see rejection on her face.

Anna drew in a deep breath and then was seated beside Raleigh, her hands reaching for the younger lady's.

"No, I'm sorry I don't. You tell us that you can't remember your name or where you're from. Doc, my husband, thinks that you were in a car accident and that you have amnesia. We'll find out where you belong." Anna held up Raleigh's left hand. "I suspect that there is someone out there desperately looking for you and that he won't stop until he does find you."

"You think that, Anna? I just want to find my home. Only I don't know where to look." Raleigh's bottom lip trembled as she fought back tears.

Anna watched her closely, sensing that this was not how Raleigh usually reacted. But it was to be expected, she decided. She looked around as she heard a tap at the door. Then the door opening before the sound of shoes hitting the boot tray sounded. Barnabas, Doc, and Dallas walked into the kitchen, heading for their mugs of coffee and sitting at the table.

Doc took one look at Raleigh and he began to pray, causing her to jump. She looked up, terror on her face before it relaxed. The other two men prayed as well.

Dallas reached for his portfolio as they finished. He needed to speak with Raleigh. This was not something that he had experienced before, interrogating someone with amnesia that complete.

"Hi. I'm Dallas." Dallas waited for Raleigh to look his way. "I'm a detective with the force here. I just need to know what you know."

Raleigh snorted, bringing grins to those with her.

"I have no idea what I know. All I know is that I can't remember my name, where I'm from, or what happened."

Dallas nodded, having already come to that conclusion from what Doc had said.

"That's okay. If I might take your photo, then I can put out a poster to the forces in the nearby towns and the county. We may be able to identify you that way."

"But what if I'm not from this area? How would you do that?" Raleigh was curious but felt somewhat disjointed from this. She didn't feel as if it was her that Dallas was talking about.

"If we don't have anyone identify you in this area, then we send the photo to the forces across the province. From there, we would reach out across the country and then outside the country. We will identify you."

"I'm sure that you will. But do I want that?" Raleigh was on her feet, heading for the room where she had awoken, dropping to the bed and pulling a blanket over her.

Doc had been on his feet, following her. He nodded at Anna as she walked by him. Raleigh was hurting in many ways. The only way for her to heal, Doc knew, was touch the hem of His garment.

Dallas turned from his desk, a frown on his face. He had sent out the photo, not really expecting a response. To have someone reach out to him from

Riverville had been unexpected. He had been unable to take the call when it came in.

"Brennan." Frankie's voice sounded loud over the phone but distracted. He was deep into an investigation and resented the interruption.

"Detective Brennan? I'm Dallas Chisholm. You responded to the found person poster that we sent out."

Frankie sat back. He knew that it was Raleigh. He just hadn't expected to find her that far from home

"I did. I know the lady. She's a friend from here. She's originally from Riverville but is living in Elmton. She's married to a friend of mine, Richard Ransome."

"Richard Ransome? He has a security team, if I remember correctly." Dallas was confused.

"He does. His team does training now instead of providing security. But Raleigh? How is she?"

"That's hard to say. Doc, a friend of mine, has examined her. She has bumps and bruises and is dehydrated. His wife found her walking on a road near here yesterday afternoon. The young lady is staying with them for now. What can you tell me about her?"

"Raleigh? As I said, she and Richard are married. They were forced to marry to save Raleigh's life. They have been trying to find the ones responsible despite abductions and assaults. Raleigh disappeared four days ago on her way home from town. Bill Butler, the investigating detective, let me know that they found her car yesterday. She had been run off the road."

---

"And that's what happened to her memory. She can't remember anything."

Frankie nodded even though Dallas could not see him.

"I would suspect that. I need to reach out to Bill and Richard."

"No, let me. I'll call them. I know Bill somewhat and I have met Richard. We'll need to bring Raleigh home." Dallas hung up from speaking with Frankie, trouble on his face. How they did that, return Raleigh to her home without further harm, troubled him. He would need to think that through.

Dallas reached for his phone once more, stopping to pray for Raleigh and then for Richard. He sensed from what Frankie had not said that the couple were in deep danger.

# Chapter 32

Standing in the chapel that was part of the Barnabas Foundation Building, Raleigh felt very much out of place. She didn't belong here, that much she knew. She just didn't know where she belonged. To say that she was scared more than she had ever been in her life was an understatement.

Anna refused to leave her side. She had introduced her to the fourteen ladies who lived in the building and the rest of the men, watching Raleigh as she responded but in a somewhat overwhelmed manner. Her arm around her, Anna drew her to a seat, watching as two little children approached them. Heath and Hannah, Brandon and Hagen's twins, were known to just throw themselves at whoever was handy to them without any thought that they might not be welcome.

Raleigh jumped as she felt the toddlers clambering up on her knee, shock on her face. Her arms surrounded them. She was not expecting the hugs and kisses that were showered on her. Turning as she heard a laughing voice speaking to the children, Raleigh studied the young lady, around her own age, she thought, before she looked over at Anna. Anna simply shrugged, her smile huge.

"I'm sorry, Raleigh. This is what Heath and Hannah do. We've tried breaking them of doing this. It just doesn't seem to work."

"It's okay, I guess." Raleigh was relieved as the children were moved to their parents' laps despite their loud protests that they needed to stay with their friend. "They're sweet."

"Thank you. They do sort of overwhelm you."

Raleigh nodded, her attention moving to the group gathering in the chapel. It wasn't just the adults. She could see some older teens as well as a number of toddlers and babies. It didn't surprise her but it did make her feel like more of an outsider than she already felt.

Buckley, the minister in the group, had his eye on Raleigh, praying for her. She was a victim of a crime, of that he was certain. He and his wife, Locklin, had left their beloved church and taken on roles in the victim support organization that had been set up by the Barnabas Foundation. He knew that Locklin had tried to speak with Raleigh earlier that day and that Raleigh had just walked away. They had to let her. They could not force her to speak with them and none of them would do that.

Dallas silently shoved the chapel door open and found a seat where he could observe Raleigh. He had spoken with Bill and agreed with him that Bill would speak with Richard. He had not heard back from either man but that didn't surprise him at all. His thoughts shifted to Buckley and his talk that evening about the healing that God provided. He knew that they all, especially, Raleigh needed that.

Early the next morning, Bill parked in front of the building. He turned to Richard, a hand resting on Richard's arm.

"We need to pray, Richard, as I know that you have been doing.  Raleigh doesn't remember anything at all from what we have been told."  Bill's eyes were full of compassion for his friend.

"I know, Bill.  It hurts.  She's been through so much lately.  Why her?"  Richard and his team had been working on the investigation, sending the information that they discovered to Lily at her request.  Emma had been silent.  That had Richard concerned.

"She has been.  And so have you.  It's wearing you down, my friend."  Bill slid from the car, watching as two men approached him.  "Barnabas.  Breck.  It's been a while."

Richard's eyes were on the building.  He just wanted to find Raleigh.  Only would she remember him?  And if she didn't remember him, would she stay with him?  That was a question he was not sure how to answer.

"Bill.  Richard.  I wish it was under different circumstances."  Barnabas pointed back towards the building.  "In here, I think.  Raleigh is with Anna and Locklin right at the moment.  We'll find them shortly."

"Thank you, fellows."  Richard sat on one of the couches in the foyer, his eyes moving around.  "This is nice.  You've planned it well."

"We have.  It's home to all of us, even though it is an office building as well."  Breck shared a look with Barnabas.  "What can we tell you, Richard?"

"Physically, Raleigh is fine?"

"She is.  Doc has examined her when she arrived and again this morning before he headed off for his shift.  It's just that she has no memory of her life or what happened to her.  He suspects that she is doing this to protect herself."

"And she will.  We've seen that before."  Richard rubbed at his face.  "What do we do to help her?  A friend from Riverville has reached out and agreed to speak with her, if she wants."

"That's what she'll need.  She'll need counselling.  Locklin, who is with her this morning, shares the responsibility of our victims' organization with her husband, Buckley.  You know them, Richard.  You know what they went through.  She is willing to continue in that role with Raleigh, if she so chooses."

"Thank you, Breck.  Now, where is she?  I just need to see my bride."  Richard was on his feet, hearing the sound of footsteps on the stairs.  He moved towards the three ladies, his eyes on Raleigh.  He waited for her to respond, to look up at him, to come to him.  He had to.  He knew that he could not force her to do that.  She had to do that of her own free will.

Raleigh had walked down the stairs, Locklin and Anna on either side of her.  She had been reluctant to do that, not sure why she was being asked to.  Her steps paused as she saw a pair of boots in her line of sight.  She had kept her eyes downcast, not wanting to see censure or dislike on anyone's face.  Her eyes raised to study the tall man in front of her.  She frowned at the welcome smile on his face. Raleigh didn't know him but he seemed familiar to her.  His hand was outstretched for hers as he patiently waited for her to make a move towards him.

Richard could hear soft conversation around him but his whole focus was on Raleigh. He decided that he would wait for however long it took for her to respond to him. His eyes showed his love for her, love that he could not verbalize, at least not yet. He didn't want to do anything that would cause her to run.

"I'm sorry. Do I know you?" Raleigh's voice was hesitant.

"You do. I'm Richard. And you are my bride." Richard noted the startled jump that she gave, understanding on his face.

"You are? I'm sorry. I don't remember. And I should." Raleigh reached for his hand at last, feeling his closing around hers in a strong and warm grip. She felt as if she had come home, except that didn't make any sense to her.

"That's okay, love. We'll work through it. We've been praying for you." Richard nodded his thanks at the group gathered around her, knowing that she was overwhelmed at the moment. He just wanted to take her home and keep her safe. Yet, he was well aware that might be difficult to do.

Raleigh turned to look back at the building as Bill drove off. He had taken a few moments to speak with the ones who gathered before he ran for his car. He was not surprised to find Richard sitting beside Raleigh in the back seat. It was what Richard did with his protectees. And Raleigh was much more precious to Richard than any protectee.

———

# Chapter 33

Walking through his house that evening, Richard was troubled.  Raleigh had been withdrawn, not what he had come to expect from her.  That hurt, he thought, as he prayed for his bride.  He had not questioned her.  That would come from Lily on the morrow.  Tonight, he just wanted to keep her safe and from harm.

Raleigh pulled the blankets up to her chin.  She was scared, that she had to admit that to herself.  Richard had talked to her, explaining what had gone on with them.  He had talked about her family, just telling that he had called them.  They wanted to see her but understood that it might be a day or so before she was ready for that. Raleigh drifted off to sleep, a prayer whispering in her heart.  She could not understand what she prayed but she was confident that God heard.

Richard reached for his phone, rubbing at the side of it before he sighed.  Rori had called earlier and he had let it go to voice mail.  Listening to it, he had heard the desperation in Rori's voice for word on his sister.

"Rori? It's Richard."  Richard waited as he heard Rori composing himself.

"Richard?  Is Raleigh with you?"  Rori was praying that she was.  He just didn't know for certain.  He stared at the television screen, watching the nature channel that he had chosen, with the sound muted. He didn't want to hear it. He just needed a distraction.

"She is, Rori. She's sleeping right now. That's the best thing for her. She's due in at the hospital tomorrow to be assessed and have any imaging done that she needs to have done."

"Thank you, Richard, for bringing her home. We need to see her. Mom and Dad need that so badly." Rori wiped at his eyes, not caring that tears flowed down his cheeks.

"We'll arrange that. She's hurting, Rori, in more ways that one. She's withdrawn, which I had expected her to be. I don't know what to say to prepare you. I did speak with the physician who examined her. He called me, just to talk. Doc simply stated that Raleigh is terrified and with that, she's withdrawn to protect herself."

"And more than likely to protect you and us." Rori got it. He knew how Raleigh would have acted had this not happened. Now, this was so uncertain with her. He didn't know what to say.

"More than likely. Listen, we see the physicians in the morning. Call me mid-afternoon. I'll see if she'll be willing to speak with you. If anything, I can update you. Tell your parents to call me, even if it's the middle of the night. I don't think that I'll be sleeping much tonight."

Richard set his phone to one side and then just crumpled forward, his face buried in his hands. He wept for his bride, knowing that this was not what they had wanted. God had allowed it, and they must walk

———

through it hand and hand.  He just prayed that she didn't walk away from him when it was all over.

Rising, he walked through his house, turning off the lights, checking that the doors and windows were locked, and stopping at the security system.  He felt uneasy that night, knowing that it was coming up to the worst part of what they faced.  Lily had called a couple of hours previously to see if Raleigh had been able to tell him anything.  His negative response was not what she had wanted to hear.

Raleigh was on her feet before the sun rose, sure that someone was in the house and after her.  She searched every room, except for Richard's bedroom, certain that she would find whoever it was.  She had stood in the hallway, watching Richard as he had slept.  Raleigh knew that she was hurting him with her responses to him.  She didn't remember him and couldn't help how she reacted.  Her eyes lived to the ceiling, pleading with God to restore her memory.  If that didn't happen, she knew that she would walk away from Richard.  Where would she go in that case?  She didn't know.  Raleigh knew that she would likely just head for another town, somewhere far away from there.

Richard roused as he heard Raleigh moving around.  He squinted at the clock through the dimness of the room.  It was too early for her to be on her feet. Yet, he could understand it.  Rising, he dressed quickly and sought to find her.  She was curled up in his office, a low light on near her, reading the papers on the wall. They had never been taken down.  Instead, the team kept adding material to them and scratched out what they had to.

Sitting nearby, Richard merely waited for Raleigh to speak. He was praying as he did so, knowing that only God would and could protect them.

"Richard? What is this on the wall?" Raleigh was on her feet at last, walking the room, reading more closely what was written.

"It's what we've discovered, love. You started it off a number of days ago. My team has just continued to work through it." Richard stifled a yawn. He was exhausted, not sleeping much in the last few days. He didn't want to make Raleigh feel responsible for what they were facing.

"I did this?" Raleigh was surprised. She had no memory of it. "What time do we have to be at the hospital today?"

"Around ten. It's okay, Raleigh. I will be with you every step of the way." Richard pledged that to her knowing that it was the truth. He would not leave her at all.

"Okay." Raleigh paused at one of the sheets of paper. "Who are these people?"

Richard walked to where she was, an arm around her. He felt her jump as he did so before she relaxed against him. This was hard, he decided, wanting to comfort her but not wanting to scare her away.

"These people? Those are your parents and your twin brother."

Raleigh stared at him, an adorable pucker between her eyebrows.

"I have parents?  And a twin brother?  I didn't know that.  When can I meet them?"  Raleigh felt hopeful that meeting them would help her to recall what she had forgotten.

"Tomorrow.  It's Saturday and they will come here.  They live not too far away in a town named Riverville.  You have a cabin near here that you inherited from a great-uncle."

"I do?"  Raleigh's face lit up.  "Can we go there today?"

"We can.  After we're done at the hospital, we'll go find your cabin.  For now, we need to find some food.  I understand that you didn't eat for a few days."

"No, I don't think that I did.  I don't remember.  I can remember two different cabins that I came to where I spent the night.  They had water there that I took."  Raleigh grew agitated. "I need to find those cabins and replace the water.  I trespassed in their homes."

"I doubt anyone would begrudge you the water or shelter.  If the doors were unlocked, it's what they expected to happen."  Richard worked away at a meal, keeping an eye on Raleigh as he did so.

Raleigh just kept opening cabinets until she found what they needed.  She stood for a moment, her hand on the pantry door, staring in at it.

"I have a pantry in my cabin.  Did we clear it out?"  Raleigh didn't see the look that Richard shot her way. She remembered something from her past without realizing it.

"We did, love. We cleared out all the food stuffs. We left it basically as you did. If you want to bring anything else back today, we can do that."

Raleigh nodded, distracted by something. She searched the main floor of the house, finding the glass angel. She reached for it, feeling the peace that it brought her. She set it back carefully on the fireplace mantle, not hearing Richard behind her until he wrapped her in his arms.

"That's important to you." His comment was not needed but she knew that he had to speak.

"It is. I just wish I knew why." She paused, a thought crossing her mind. "Richard? Do we have guardian angels?"

"I firmly believe that we do. You're asking for a reason." Once more, he patiently waited for her to sort through her thoughts and speak.

"I am. I felt someone with me when I was walking. I was not alone. But I couldn't see anyone."

"God does that, love. He provides angels to protect us. Sometimes they're visible. Other times, they're not."

# Chapter 34

Walking towards Raleigh's cabin that late morning, Richard was on high alert. His team had appeared and then scattered to provide cover for them. Raleigh's hand was tight in Richard's. She wondered at that and then just shrugged. They were married. Perhaps, this is what he always did.

She hesitated as she approached the cabin, suddenly stopping. Raleigh could not lift a foot to take another step forward. Richard's gaze centred on her and then the cabin. He sighed to himself. Something had stopped her. He simply turned her around and walked back to his truck where he tucked her inside. Stephen approached him as he did so.

"Richard? What just happened? Aren't you going into the cabin?"

"No, we're not. There's something off there that Raleigh senses. We've been through this too many times to ignore that. Pull our team back out." Richard's phone was out as he called for help.

Two hours later, Bill walked back from the cabin, anger growing inside him. This had gone too far, he decided. He had arrived with patrol officers. On searching around the cabin, they had discovered freshly-turned earth. That had resulted in the bomb squad being called. Instead of a bomb, though, they had found a body.

---

"Bill?  I don't like the look on your face." Richard leaned again the hood of his truck, angled in such a way so that he could still see Raleigh.

"No, I don't like it either."  Bill's words were clipped and fast.  "We need you to leave and leave now.  I've called in the medical examiner."

Richard's movements ceased.  For Bill to call in the medical examiner?  That meant a body.

"How recent?"  Richard's own words were clipped as he too struggled with anger and an attempt to understand what had happened.

"In the last day, we think.  That lets Raleigh off the hook.  She was not in town.  And now, we need to call in someone to protect you two."

"We do.  My team will work during the week days.  Don and Abe are freeing up some of their men to work overnight and the weekends. Just pray that this is over soon."  Richard spun and stalked around his truck, inside it before Bill could say another word.  He now needed to find the words to tell Raleigh what had been found.

"Richard?  I don't like the look on your face. What did they find?"  Raleigh's voice was very quiet, almost too quiet to be heard.

"A body buried in the back yard, Raleigh.  We'll need to leave.  Bill has ordered us to.  I'm sorry.  I had prayed that it would be different."

"I know that you did.  It is what it is."  Raleigh was philosophical about what they had found.  "Now what?"

———

"Now what?  We head home.  My team moves in to protect us.  And Don and Abe are sending some of their teams to work the overnight hours and the weekends until we find out who it is.  And we will find them and bring them to justice.  I promise you that."  Richard didn't continue.  If he had, he would have told her that he would do that, even if it meant his death.  He didn't think that she needed to hear that.

Raleigh paced the office building that Richard had headed to.  She knew that his team was there, meeting with him.  She hated this, she decided, hated that she could not remember who she was or where she was from.  Her steps took her towards the conference room, to stand outside the door where she could not be seen.  She listened to the conversation among the team, realizing how well that they worked together.  Raleigh felt as if she was a disruptive force.

Jumping as she felt a hand on her arm, Raleigh's own hand covered her mouth to prevent a scream.  Silver stood there, having come to find Raleigh.  The team wanted her in on the decisions, knowing that if they didn't, she just might run on them.  And if she did, then Richard would follow her.  That would put them both at a greater risk than they already were.

"Raleigh?  Are you okay?  I didn't mean to frighten you."  Silver reached to hug Raleigh before she turned her to the conference room.  "We need you in on this."

"No, I shouldn't be.  It's not what I do.  I know that."  Raleigh moved forward reluctantly, Richard on his feet with his hand outstretched for her.

"No, it's not what you do, love.  But we want you to be part of the planning.  You need to take back control of some aspects of your life. Right now, you're floundering just because you can't remember.  We understand that."  Richard seated her before he sat beside her, a hand reaching for hers once more. "Timothy had a thought and wanted to speak with you"

Raleigh's eyes turned to Timothy, a frown on her face for a moment.

"What did you think about, Timothy?"  Her voice was quiet and monotone, not what they knew her to be.

"Raleigh, Bill was around when you were up at the house.  He is very concerned about what they found.  They have identification on the body all ready, but he needs to confirm some information.  Then, he'll meet with you and Richard.  I know this is difficult. Have you remembered anything at all?"

Raleigh stared at him and then around at each of the ones seated at the table.  She knew that they were praying for her.  She had been assured of that fact.

"Not really.  I just remember feeling that someone was with me when I was walking.  I didn't see anyone.  Is there some way to track my path?"

"I have a friend working back through that with his dog.  You met Bradon when you were at the Barnabas Foundation building."  Stephen nodded at her look of surprise.  "He does search and rescue as well as evaluating dogs. Anna took him to about where she found you.  He volunteered to do that.  One of Abe's men and one of Don's men are working with him."

———

"I see. I'm causing a lot of trouble and work for everyone."

"Not really. It's what we do, love." Richard hastened to assure her. "And we are looking out for our families. They will have protection with them if they need to. And if we have to move them somewhere safe, that will be done."

Raleigh nodded, her head dropping to Richard's shoulder. She was exhausted from everything, just wanting to sleep. Richard gave a soft sound and then was on his feet, his keys handed to Naomi before he swept Raleigh into his arms and headed for the house. He turned from the couch in his office, taking with thanks the blanket Silver handed him.

"I guess that ends our meeting, Naomi. Thank you. You four work through what you need to. Call who you need to. My focus is on Raleigh."

"As it should be. When do you meet with her family?" Naomi was concerned about a lot of traffic coming in and out of the area.

"Tomorrow. It's Saturday. Abe and a couple of his team will be here. You four take off. If I need to, then I'll call."

Naomi reached to hug her friend before she walked away. She was deeply troubled, knowing that it was coming to a head, as they say, but not knowing who to look for. The ones after Richard and Raleigh were staying too hidden.

# Chapter 35

The next day, Raleigh stood in the office doorway, listening to the voices of the couple and the young man who were greeting Richard. She shook for a moment, knowing that she had to meet them, but terrified to do so. She just didn't know why.

Ross and Rebekah hesitated before they headed for the office. Rori had hung back to speak with Richard, their voices too low for anyone else to hear them. They watched as Raleigh backed away, not coming towards them as she usually did. This was not their daughter.

Raleigh was not comfortable meeting her family. They could all see that. Her parents and Rori left after a few awkward hours. She had not been able to talk much with them. Richard and Rori had borne the burden of conversation, knowing that Raleigh was unsettled. It distressed them all but not one of them could change it.

Richard stood in the kitchen, rubbing at the back of his neck. He had no idea where the investigation stood. Lily had not updated him and they both needed that. Raleigh was with him, but not with him, if that made any sense. She was working away at a meal for them, but he could tell that her thoughts were elsewhere.

"What are you thinking, love?" Richard reached past her for the coffee carafe in order to pour their drinks.

Raleigh shrugged, her eyes on the salad that she was tossing.

"I don't know.  I didn't recognize them.  That hurt them.  When will I, Richard?"  Raleigh was hoping against hope that Richard could give her a timeline.

"We don't know that, love.  It may take a sudden shock to help you remember.  It may come in bits and pieces.  Even then, there may be things that you will never remember.  I'm praying, as are our friends, that your memory comes back quickly.  The physician did say that could happen."

Raleigh nodded, knowing that Richard spoke correctly.

"I just want my memory back.  It's not fair to you.  It's not fair to anyone else."  Raleigh threw a cloth across the room in anger before she crumpled to the floor, sobs shaking her body.

Richard was startled for a moment, his eyes following the path of the cloth.  He was seated on the floor within seconds, Raleigh gathered into his arms, weeping as she sobbed. He could not make it better for her no matter how much he wanted that. He could only hold her when she wept. He grew angrier than he had ever been. Someone was hurting the one person who he adored and loved more than his own life. He wanted this over with and over with then.

Worn out with her weeping, Raleigh slept, her head on Richard's shoulder.  He sat for the longest time, his anger burning before he began to pray, turning his anger over to the Lord.  He knew that he had to.

Rising carefully with Raleigh in his arms, he simply walked to his office, tucking her under a blanket on the couch. He returned to the kitchen, staring at their meal before it was back in the fridge. He reached for his mug of coffee, stalking back to his office. He was determined to find an answer and find it that night.

Bill tapped at Richard's door an hour later. He shrugged at Lily as they waited for Richard to answer. They had news for the couple. They just didn't like what they had to tell them.

Richard shut the door behind them, knowing that they would not be there at that time of the evening unless they had some information for them. He pointed towards the office.

"In there. Raleigh is sleeping. I will not awaken her unless it is absolutely necessary. She had a meltdown after her parents and brother were here." Richard looked ragged, the stress showing on his face and in how he was moving.

Bill studied his friend, shaking his head. God was there, he knew, protecting Richard and Raleigh and giving them the strength that they needed.

"Richard? Before we start, let me pray with you as a friend. Then, Lily needs to give you some information. She's the one working on the investigation. I am here just for support for both you and Raleigh."

"Have you solved this?" Richard's grim look didn't soften.

"We'll talk, Richard.  First, though, we need to pray.  And pray hard.  This is where it gets hard, as you well know."

Richard raised his head thirty minutes later, feeling refreshed.  His gaze went to Raleigh, seeing that she was still sleeping, her sleep troubled he could tell by her movements.

"Okay, Lily.  What do you have to tell me?"

"First, we are working through this as quickly as we can.  Emma has provided multiple leads for us that we eliminating or confirming.  That is good news in that we're working more quickly that way.

"Next, the grave at her cabin.  She didn't have any security cameras that we know of.  And I'm not sure that she would even remember if she did, given her amnesia.  We have identified the man who was buried there.  He was not local to here.  He had arrest warrants out for him on the other side of the province. He was a hit man."

Richard sat up straighter.

"A hit man?  He was taken out?  But by whom?"

"That's what we haven't confirmed as of yet. We are working through it as you know that we will. Now, the evidence does suggest that he was killed elsewhere and brought there."

"A plot?  A plot to frame Raleigh?"  Richard sat back, his eyes closing for a moment.

"That's what it looks like. Either that or a threat." Bill spoke up.  "We've seen that before, Richard.  Each one of us has.  Now, what do you have to tell us?"

Richard frowned for a moment before he was on his feet, heading for the table on the other side of the room. He paused to watch Raleigh for a moment before he was back in his chair.

"Here. This is what the team has come up with. I've been working on a different angle. I'm still pulling data and have to work it through before I pass it on to you."

Bill and Lily read through the material, both nodding at the concise and complete summary that they had been handed.

"This part? About her hometown? What did Stephen mean?" Lily looked up at that, her finger marking her spot on the page.

"Her hometown? She's been watched there. Frankie confirmed that. She was watched from her youth. And he can't get a handle on why. He is identifying suspects and will work with you on that, Lily. He thought he might have more information by tomorrow for you."

"I'll call him. That will work. Now, what more can you tell us?"

Richard drew in a deep breath and then began to speak, his eyes on Bill as he did so. Bill's face whitened at the name that Richard had given him.

Shaking her head, Raleigh walked away from Richard, heading for the outside. She needed to be outside. She had been inside for too long, she decided.

Tate and Shanli shared a look before they followed after her. They knew to some extent how she was feeling. Walking around the yard, they simply linked arms with her, remaining silent as they did so.

"Ladies, how do we get my memory back?" Raleigh was tired of not knowing who she was or who her family was.

"That's difficult to know how to do that. It's not something that we can just hit you over the head and restore it." Shanli grinned at her.

"I know. There has to be some way to do that." Raleigh stopped walking, staring straight ahead.

"What would you like to do, then?" Tate knew that Raleigh was wanting to do something other than just sit back and let life happen.

"I need to retrace where I've been in town. I need to go back to the cabin, as much as I don't want to." Raleigh turned back towards the house, seeing all the men and Silver and Naomi walking towards them. "We have company, ladies."

"That we do. I wonder what they have discovered." Tate moved towards Timothy, finding him wrapping her into his arms.

"Raleigh?  You're troubled."  Richard stood in front of her, reaching for her hands.

"I am.  I want to walk back through town, to where you say that I work, to the church, and to the cabin."

"We can do that. That's what we've decided that we need to do.  We'll start with church in the morning. Then, we head for Ev's diner.  From there, we'll go wherever it is that you need and want to go."

Raleigh nodded, knowing that Richard had planned this, working to ensure that she would be as safe as she could be and that his team had made plans to keep both of them safe.

"That's fine, Richard.  Now, these people need to go and do something fun.  We'll meet at church, correct?"  Raleigh was making steps to try and take back her life.

"We will do that.  Stay safe, you two."  The group walked away, leaving Richard in front of Raleigh, her hands still in his.

"What do you wish to do, Raleigh?"  Richard waited patiently for her to speak.  Whatever her decision was, he would back her. He simply prayed for his lady, begging God for a resolution of this.  He didn't know if they could go through much more and survive.

The next morning, Raleigh shifted closer to Richard, finding his arm around her.  She was unsettled, knowing that they were under observation. And that observation was not from their friends.  She frowned before she reached for Richard's hand, drawing his attention back to her.

"Richard? Can we leave? I don't feel safe here."

Richard was on his feet, leading from the sanctuary. Timothy and Stephen were with them, watching closely. Naomi and Silver moved quickly to the outside.

Don and two of his men waited for Richard to move towards his truck before Don was on the move, stopping Richard's forward walk.

"Wait, Richard. Let us take you home. I don't know that your truck would be safe."

Richard stared at his vehicle, knowing that Don was correct.

"Thank you, Don. I'll have an officer go over it. Raleigh, I'm sorry. Don will drive us home."

Raleigh had frozen in place as Don spoke. She frowned at him.

"I know you." Raleigh was struggling with her memory.

"You do, Raleigh. I had an aunt in hospice. You were there for her."

Raleigh continued to stare at him before she nodded at him.

"How do I remember you and not something else? I don't understand that."

"That's what happens, Raleigh." Richard had been listening with interest to the exchange between Don and Raleigh.

"It does. Now, how be we get you two out of sight?" Don pointed towards his SUV. "In there."

Don's eyes were on the move as Paul drove away. He felt the presence of someone watching them. He just couldn't find that person.

"How do we do this, Richard? How do we find them? They're out there. It's as if they are listening in on everything that we say."

"I know that they're not. I think it's someone close to us, someone who we would not expect. And I don't know who." Richard was at a loss.

Paul shared a look with Don, who nodded. They had discussed this as a team, searching for a name. They had come with a couple and passed them on to Lily. She had looked at Paul as he stood in front of her, the piece of paper extended out to her.

"You said who?" Lily had been shocked, to put it mildly. The name was not who she expected.

Paul nodded, knowing that they had just opened up the investigation in a way that was unexpected.

"It's who we think. Don's from this town. He's Richard's friend from childhood. He knows the town well."

"I know that he does. It doesn't make it any easier, you know." Lily walked away as Paul laughed before he sobered. This was not where they wanted the investigation to go.

# Chapter 37

The following Saturday, Raleigh stared out at the pouring rain.  She had wanted to be outside, working in the gardens.  That was not happening. Richard had to have been at a meeting, reluctant to leave her on her own.  She had shrugged her shoulders, not willing to admit how scared that she was to be on her own.

Spinning at a sudden sound at the door, Raleigh searched for a place to hide.  She heard the thundering at the door and then the hammering as something kept slamming into it.  Running for the basement stairs, she ran across the floor, sliding in behind some stacked boxes, crouching down and pulling a blanket over herself.

Hearing the sounds of heavy, hurried footsteps overhead, Raleigh hardly dared to breathe.  She prayed for safety, trusting that God would provide that protection for her.  She didn't dare move even when the footsteps died away.

Richard approached his house, sensing something that off.  He parked and then headed for the front door.  Coming to a sudden halt, he stared at the broken door before he was on the run, hunting for Raleigh.  Not finding her at first, he spun around, before he headed back to the basement.  He started a systemic search, approaching the boxes.  He frowned as he saw the blanket, not remembering seeing it there.  It was one that was usually in his office.

Reaching for it, Richard touched it, jumping slightly as it moved.  Pulling it back, he stared at

Raleigh as she huddled in as small as crouch as she could.  Raleigh jumped as his hand touched her, a scream coming from her.  She scrambled away, her hands over her head, not realizing that it was not the men after her.

Richard's hand stopped before he began to pray audibly and then began to sign the hymns and choruses that he loved.  He sat, his eyes not moving from Raleigh even as he heard footsteps overhead and heard voices calling his name.

Riley and Rori had appeared, worried about the couple.  The sight of the broken door had frightened them, driving them to search.  Rori had headed back outside to look.  Riley made his way at last down to the basement, pausing as he heard Richard's voice. He moved forward carefully, stopping as Richard's hand was raised.  He didn't want to make matter worse.

Raleigh gradually raised her head, disoriented for a moment.  Hearing Richard's voice, she searched for him.  Seeing him, she threw herself towards him, finding his arms wrapping around her.  She sobbed, the terror of the past weeks driven from her. She couldn't stop her sobs.

Rori had returned, heading for the group as he heard Raleigh's sobs.  He didn't think that he had ever hear her weep like that.  Riley moved backwards, beckoning him with him and pointing to the stairs

"Riley?  What's going on?"  Rori paced around the table, his eyes moving frequently towards the basement door.

"I don't know, Rori. I know that Richard found her. I don't know what's happened. She's been frightened and frightened badly." Riley reached for the coffee pot, setting coffee for them. "He'll be up with her when he can. For now, we need to call the authorities."

Lily walked around the house, frowning at the disturbance that could be seen. It was obvious that many attempts had been made to enter the house, the front door taking the brunt of the assault. Adam, a friend who was a carpenter, was on site, waiting to install a new door for them.

Richard sat up, his eyes on Raleigh.

"Raleigh, love, what happened?"

"I heard someone and hid. Did you catch them?" Raleigh rubbed her hands together, shivering as if she was very cold.

"No, I don't think so. I found the door broken open and had to hunt for you." He reached for the blanket. "I don't understand how this got down here."

Raleigh shrugged. She wasn't sure either.

"I thought it was in the office." She looked up, a smile lighting up her face. "God. He did this."

"He did." Richard stood, his hand reaching for hers. "I think that we need to leave. I'm sure that Riley has already called in the authorities."

"He's here?" Raleigh almost ran towards the stairs. "I need to see him. Where's Rori?"

———

"I don't know where he is." Richard stared after her before he was on the move. "Raleigh? What just happened?"

"Richard? What do you mean?" Raleigh ran up the stairs, hunting for Rori. She didn't see the astonished looks sent her way. She was intent on finding Rori.

Rori turned as he heard running footsteps, bracing himself just in time as Raleigh threw herself at him.

"Rori? You're safe. I was so worried about you." She hugged him before she turned, finding Riley staring at her as if he had seen a ghost. She reached to hug him as well before running for Richard as he walked rapidly towards them. "Richard? What day is it? I feel as if I've lost some time."

"And you have. Quite a few days." Richard hugged, praising God that Raleigh was remembering. "And you have remembered."

"I am? Why? Had I forgotten something?" She couldn't understand why he was speaking as he was.

"You did. You had amnesia, love. You couldn't remember any of us." Richard stared down at her. Before he could even stop himself, he kissed her, finding her responding.

"I didn't? I don't remember that." Raleigh struggled to release herself from Richard's arm spinning in a circle. "Lily? What's going on?" She moved rapidly towards her, finding Lily staring at her in turn.

"Someone broke into your home. I understand that you found a hiding place." Lily grinned at her friend.

"I did. And I want to know why that blanket was down there. None of us moved it there." Raleigh walked away, leaving everyone staring after her.

# Chapter 38

Bill stared at Lily later that afternoon, not comprehending what she was saying. Lily repeated herself, a grin on her face.

"She remembered? Just like that?" Bill was astounded.

"She did. The fright that she underwent when the men broke in was enough to break through the barriers that were erected. Now, we need to find out who it was that broke in. They disabled the security system somehow. We don't know where or how. It was not on Richard's property."

"Someone hacked in?" At Lily's nod, Bill rubbed at his cheek. "Talk to Noah. See if he can figure out where they hacked in. He should be able to." Noah, a friend of theirs, was an ethical hacker. Bill trusted that he would search until he found out where it had been hacked.

"I'll talk to him and then have him contact Richard. This is where it gets so dangerous for them."

"It always does, Lily. It always does. Have you found any more information about that name Paul gave you?" Bill walked with Lily towards her office.

"Emma was working on that. She had already found the name and knew that he was involved." Lily dropped her jacket on her desk chair.

"Keep working on it, Lily. Each little bit of information either confirms or eliminates something."

———

"I know. It's just that it's Richard. It shouldn't be him. He gives and gives and gives of himself to others."

"He does, Lily." Bill perched himself on the corner of her desk. "It's how life works, Lily. God allows things to happen to Christians as well as non-Christians. We don't get special treatment. But He does protect us. It's just not always how we expect it to happen."

"I know that. However, it still sucks big time." Lily sat, reaching to wake up her computer. "If you think of anything that would help, let me know. I can use all the help that I can find."

Richard roused in the night, hearing whimpering. He was on his feet, running for Raleigh, finding her sitting up, her arms wrapped around her head. He was sitting beside her, wrapping her in his arms. He began to pray, desperation in it.

Raleigh began to sob, totally inconsolable. Richard begged God to ease her panic, knowing that He would. It might just take time but it would happen.

Raleigh began to calm down at last, her arms hugging Richard. Her head went down against him. She listened to his heart beating.

"Okay, love?" Richard's voice was low but calm.

"Getting there. Richard, when will it be over?" Raleigh wanted to return to her life, without a threat hanging over them.

"Soon, I pray, love. Lily called me after you went to bed. They were given another name to investigate. She said it was high on the list of people, near the top. Just not the top one."

"I'm glad." Raleigh yawned, her eyes closing as she slept.

Richard watched her sleep, a soft smile on his face. His love for her was deepening each day. He just didn't know how she felt. When this was over, he planned on a heart-to-heart with her.

Morning seemed to come too soon. Richard headed for the office building, yawning as he did so. He had not slept the night before. Instead, he had found the chair in Raleigh's bedroom, wrapped them both in a blanket, and just sat, holding her all night. He had spent the night in prayer, waiting for God to speak. He had heard God speaking in his heart. He had to obey what had been asked of him.

Raleigh watched him walk away, knowing that he had made plans. He had told her that he had but that he needed to refine them with his team. Then, they would talk with her. She would not be left out. Raleigh just hoped that it would be a plan to bring down whoever it was and soon. She knew that neither one of them would be able to take much more.

Prowling the office building, Richard heard the team in for training speaking with his team. They all headed for the training building, leaving Richard on his own. He didn't like that Raleigh was by herself. He ran for the house, a grin on his face as he tugged her with him back to the office. Shanli and Tate had shown up, wanting to know what they could do. They informed Richard that Sorley and Nollan would be there as well. It was time to make plans.

Lily walked through the office that afternoon, finding everyone gathered in the conference room, working away. There was soft laughter at times. Lily frowned at that. There was not a sense of rushing any more. It was as if they knew that it was almost over and that the culprits would soon be in custody.

Raleigh walked up behind Lily, an arm hugging her.

"Lily? You're here. With good news?"

"I think we have some good news. What is going on here? It sounds more like a party than work."

"We're making it into a party. There's been enough doom and gloom. So, we're working it with a positive spirit. It was too hard the other way."

Lily nodded, her eyes thoughtful.

"That comes from you, Raleigh. You bring that to your work and to your clients. You see enough doom and gloom as you call it. A positive spirit and happiness get you through so much."

Richard stood with his arms wrapped around his bride, nodding as he listened to Lily.

"It does, Lily. We see that in Proverbs. Barnabas was an encourager, and that's what we're trying to be. And when we look at David and what he went through? He still praised God through it all. We can no less."

"And we are told to rejoice in all things." Lily nodded, understanding what Richard was saying.

"We are. Now, why do you have to tell us?" Richard grinned at her, looking younger than he had for weeks.

# Chapter 39

The next day, Richard and Raleigh walked the main street of Elmton in the late afternoon. There had not been a team in for training that week. They were heading for Ev's diner, determined to take back their life. This was the start of it.

"Someone is watching us, love." Richard was on alert, his eyes searching for whoever it was.

"Of course, they are. They always do. This is what they call crunch time, isn't it?" Raleigh paused to stare into a small shop. "Richard, can we go in here? I love this shop. It always brings comfort and peace when I enter it."

Richard nodded, knowing that the owner was a member of their church. Sally, the owner, was a strong Christian, willing to help anyone. He always told her that she was the hands and feet of Christ in their town. She just laughed at him. Raleigh walked through the store, searching for something. She reached for a glass rainbow, recognizing it as being made by a friend.

"This is made by a friend, Richard. She does such beautiful work."

"I have always loved looking at her work." He reached for it. "You need this, Raleigh. You need a visible promise that God loves you and promises not to let you go through this kind of flood again."

She smiled up at him, amazed again at his height.

"Thank you, Richard. That is how I feel. I have just never expressed it that way." Raleigh reached to hug him, her eyes turning towards another object. She reached for it. The glass heart was just what she wanted. "And this is you, Richard. You have opened up your heart to me and helped me to open mine."

Richard stood, stunned at her words. He hadn't realized that was how she felt

They walked from the shop, stopping for Richard to tuck the parcels in his truck. He then reached for her hand, heading for Ev's diner. Raleigh sparkled with happiness that morning, making her even more beautiful, Richard thought.

Old George watched them from a doorway near the diner. He had received word that a new hitman was in town and had that couple in his sights. He had approached Lily but he had no identification to tell her. She had nodded, thanked him, and then asked for what other information that he found. He had walked away, keeping to the character that he had lived in for so many months. Bill was right. He needed to come in from the streets.

Seating Raleigh, Richard slid into a seat across from her. He grinned as she teased him, just happy that her memory had returned. He sobered as he felt danger approaching them.

Raleigh watched him closely, seeing him shift to work mode as he called it. She sighed, knowing that their day had likely changed.

"Richard, what happened? Who did you see?"

"I didn't see anyone, love. It's just a feeling that we're being watched and that danger is approaching us very quickly. I don't know that we would have time to react." Richard shook his head as she opened her mouth to speak. "We'll eat, love, and then we'll head home."

"That isn't fair. We need this over." Raleigh reached for the menu although she already knew what she wanted.

"It's not. We just have to remember that God is in control." Richard reached for her hands, his head bowing as he prayed for them.

Avery watched them from where he stood at the cash desk. He was deeply worried about his friend. He too had word that a new hitman was in town. He walked towards them with their meals, a frown on his face.

Richard looked up, reading Avery's face.

"You have news, Avery." It was a statement, not a question.

"I do, Richard. There's a new hitman in town. We just don't have a confirmed identification of him. And trust me, we're working on that. Word is that the hitman is from outside the country."

"A stranger? And there are many strangers around town for the festival this weekend." Richard sat back, a troubled look on his face. "It's the weekend. I'm not calling in my team."

"You'll have to, Richard. We need to tuck you two away somewhere for a few days." Avery walked away.

Raleigh's eyes shifted from Richard to where she could see Avery.

"It's coming up to that time, isn't it? The time when we meet whoever it is that is after us?" Raleigh waited until Richard nodded. "We've expected this, Richard. We've talked about it together and with your team. We can't prevent it. It's going to happen. As you have said so many times, we need to trust God to protect us."

"I know, love. We do need to do that. It's hard to see you threatened." Richard reached for her hands once more to ask the blessing on their food. As he sat back, movement across the room caught his attention. *No,* he decided, *I don't know that person. But he's very interested in us. Lord, protect us as we leave.*

Tucking Raleigh into his truck, Richard turned in a circle. They were being stalked, he knew, the danger growing closer to them. He had no idea how to avoid it. Timothy had sent a text, simply stating that the team would be at their place. Where were they?

Heading for home, Richard kept close watch around them. There was a vehicle following them. As he turned into his driveway, the lights flashed on the patrol car. Richard drew a deep breath. A patrol vehicle had followed them.

Raleigh looked for a spot for her new rainbow, deciding to set it beside her angel. Her hand lingered on the angel, a sense of peace flowing through her. It was almost over.  She could feel God's hand on her that day, a feeling of protection growing in her heart.

Richard stood in his office, a grin on his face.  He reached for the heart that Raleigh had left there.  She had grinned at him as he hugged her.  Richard turned his head for a moment, eying the door, knowing that his team was almost there.  He walked towards her, sweeping her into his arms and kissing her.  He could not help himself.

"I love you, Raleigh.  Thank you for being who you are."

Raleigh stood frozen for a moment, her fingers on her lips, a look of wonder on her face.  She was loved and knew that she loved him in return.

# Chapter 40

Timothy and Stephen walked the outside of the house, feeling danger moving towards their boss. They didn't like it but knew that they could not prevent it. Timothy headed away from Stephen, searching along the edge of the property and heading for the training facility. A soft sound reached him, causing him to spin towards it. He didn't see the man who had risen from the shrubbery, a gun raised to knock him out. Stephen was quickly bound and gagged before being dragged away and hidden from view.

Timothy moved around the property, a frown on his face as he realized that he had not seen Stephen for a few moments. That was not how they worked. His pace rapid, he walked that way, not finding his team mate. He too heard a soft sound and was down before he could react. Unable to fight his attacker, he was bound and gagged and dragged to a spot near Stephen. His head hit the ground again, his eyes memorizing as much as he could about his attacker.

Naomi and Silver were in the house with Richard and Raleigh. They had insisted on that. The doors were locked. They had a deep sense of danger, Richard agreeing with them. They had not heard from Timothy and Stephen and that worried them.

"Where are they, Silver?" Naomi peeked out the window towards the back of the property. "I don't see them."

"I know. I don't like it. We should be able to see them." Silver paced away to peek through other windows. "Richard? We haven't heard from Timothy or Stephen. And we can't see them."

Richard nodded, a grim look on his face. He had expected something like this. He prayed that the men on his team were still alive.

Raleigh wrapped her arms around herself, praying for Richard's team. She was afraid, more afraid than she had ever been. She knew that this was it. She could only pray for safety for them all.

The men who had taken down Timothy and Stephen approached their leader. He pointed silently towards the house before they crept that way. Knowing that the house was well secured, they had been prepared. A hacker friend of theirs had taken down the security system once more, not knowing that Noah had identified him and that police officers were on his doorstep to arrest him.

Surrounding the house, the six men waited. They crept closer as quickly as they could at a word from their leader. It would be difficult to breach the house, but they had orders to do just that. Battering rams hammered at the doors before they were broken in. Searching the house, they turned to one another. No one was in the house. They had not seen anyone leave. So, where were they?

Richard had caught movement of one of the men, realizing that Timothy and Stephen would not likely be of any help. Their safety was on his shoulders. He grabbed for Raleigh's hand, calling for Silver and Naomi to come with them. Their feet pounded down the stairs to the basement before Richard reached for a certain beam. A door opened up before he shoved Raleigh into the tunnel, Naomi and Silver following. He listened as he heard the hammering at the doors before he too was behind the closed door.

Naomi ran down the tunnel, knowing that it came out near the training building. Silver followed her, Raleigh between Silver and Richard. They did not say a word, just ran for the opening. Naomi slid to a halt, her weapon out as she scanned the area before she nodded. The four ran for the woods, sliding once more to a halt as they heard a sound. Richard moved that way cautiously, his weapon back in its holster as he reached to free both Timothy and Stephen. They nodded at the question on his face before they were running towards the ladies and then running from Richard's home. They had to. They needed to get the couple to safety and running away was the only option.

Patrol vehicles streamed onto Richard's property, their red and blue lights sending crazy patterns across the buildings. The men who had been sent to take Richard and Raleigh were instead taken away themselves.

Lily approached the house, searching for Richard and not finding him. Her phone vibrated before she checked the text message, breathing a sigh of relief. Richard and Raleigh were safe and on the move. His team was with him.

Heading for the office, Lily searched for either Bill or Andrew. She found neither man. A frustrated groan came from her. She needed to speak with either one but couldn't at the moment. Instead, she buried herself into the paperwork that was piling up on her desk.

Bill and Andrew found her an hour later, simply approaching her office and then sitting, waiting for her to speak.

"Lily?" Andrew's voice had her head raising. "What do you know?"

"Not a lot. We've arrested the men who broke into Richard's home. Adam will need to replace both doors this time. Richard was able to get away. He's on the move with Raleigh and his team. I don't know where exactly they are. I would suspect somewhere in his neighbourhood. Only they're on foot."

"On foot? Yes, they would be." Andrew thought through the consequences of that. "I'll send out an unmarked car. They'll watch for the group." Andrew was on his feet, moving towards the desk sergeant.

"Lily? What else?" Bill knew that there was more that Lily had not yet said.

"His security system was hacked again. Noah was waiting for that, found the address, and I sent in officers. That man is now in one of our cells as are the men who invaded Richard's home. We're starting the interviews, but somehow I don't think anyone will speak."

"Not likely. Their families are safe?"

"They are. Don moved in on Richard's parents and brother when this came down. I spoke with Abe and he was doing the same for Raleigh's parents and brother. I want this over, Bill, and over today."

"And how close are we to that?" Bill wanted the same thing.

"Very close. I have one bit of information to confirm before I head over for the search and arrest warrants."

"Good. Come and find me." Bill stood for a moment. "You've done well, Lily. This has been an unusual case without much information for us to investigate. You've managed to do that." He walked away, not seeing the surprise and then the smile on Lily's face.

# Chapter 41

Richard's feet finally stopped moving as he wrapped an arm around his bride. She leaned against him, fatigue taking her strength for the moment. They had been on the move for the last thirty moments, Raleigh just not knowing where they were heading. His team scattered, scanning the area for anyone who meant them harm. Richard's own eye scanned the buildings near them, knowing that they would provide shelter for the moment.

"Richard? We're downtown?" Raleigh's voice was soft.

"We are. We'll find shelter here for now. And then I'll get word to Lily or Bill. I know that the people down here will protect us as well as they can." Richard was on the move again, Raleigh's hand tight in his.

His team surrounded them, moving them quickly into a building. Old George looked around as they did so, having expected them at some point.

"Richard?" Old George walked towards him.

"Old George? We're on the run and need your help." Richard walked towards him as well, taking the bottles of water handed to him and then handed them to the others.

"I can see that. I expected this. I'll contact Lily or Bill for you. For now, find somewhere in here to hide with your team. I'll keep watch." His keen eyes watched Raleigh. She was wearing down, he could see.

"Thank you, Old George." Richard was aware that the other man was an officer. He had discovered that one day and had promised to keep the secret. "My home was broken into this morning. We were able to escape. That is how we ended up here."

Lily reached for her phone, hearing the chime for a text message. She was on her feet, feeling relief at word that Richard and Raleigh were safe.

"Bill? They're safe." Lily had tracked him down in the break room. "Old George came through with a text."

"He did? And that's good. He'll keep them hidden until we can find him and then bring them in." Bill was on the move, his coffee forgotten. "Where do we stand with the warrants?"

"Ready to serve. Our teams are discussing strategy at the moment. Jason's in charge of that."

"Good. I'll find him. You're still working through something." Bill didn't question her, merely stating that fact.

"I am, Bill. I am. This is almost over for them. I don't want to miss anyone." She looked up as she heard her name. "And Abe and Emma are here. What do you two have for us?"

Emma held up a folder.

"We need to go over this and now. I have tracked down the reason and the person responsible. It's not who we think, although he is in the chain of command for all this."

"It's not?" Lily reached for the folder, flipping through the paperwork. "You're right, Emma. Old George told me this name. And that's what I was working on. She's not in town at the moment."

"She's in town. She'll be hiding somewhere." Abe walked away with Bill after making his statement.

"He's right, you know." Emma grinned at Lily before she sobered. "How do we find her?"

"Old George. He'll know where she is. He's already watching for her." Lily's phone was out as her fingers flew across the keyboard. She stuffed the phone back into a pocket. "Okay, Emma. Let's find her. Where would you hide?"

"In plain sight." Emma was on the move, heading for the outside, Lily grabbing for her jacket before she followed.

"Exactly. Now, where would in plain sight be in this town?" Lily paced beside Emma, her thoughts troubled for a moment before her face cleared. "And I know exactly where that would be." Her phone was out as she asked for a patrol vehicle to head for the house near Richard's home.

Emma nodded. That's where she would have been, right near her prey. That way, she could keep track of their movements.

"You've thought that someone has been very close to him all along."

"That's correct. They haven't received the threats by mail or parcel. Not a one. That told us that whoever it was kept too close an eye on them."

————

"And your thoughts were correct." Emma paused. "There's someone else, isn't there?"

"There is. And that man is from your town. He's related to her, I think." Lily blew out a breath. "I need to talk to Frankie."

"Frankie was muttering something last night about making an arrest this morning. He had a patrol car sitting outside the man's home, keeping him from leaving. I would suspect that by now, the arrest has been made."

"I pray that it has been. It will take some of the pressure off of us but in the same instance put more on us to find this woman. I won't call her a lady. She's definitely not that."

Emma laughed at the fierce expression on Lily's face and at her words.

"No, she's not. Now, where would you go if you left that house and came to the downtown area?"

"Ev's diner." Lily headed that way. Instead of entering through the normal door, she walked in the kitchen door, heading for the edge of the kitchen. She stood to one side, scanning the diner. "And she's here. For now, she's on her own." Lily's phone was out once more, asking for help. She opened her email as the chime came, nodding. She had the arrest warrant that she had asked for. "I have the warrant. Help is on the way. Ev? I'm about to arrest someone in your diner. You may want to clear out your customers and staff."

Ev stared at her for a moment, before she nodded.

"How long?"

"May be fifteen minutes. I am just waiting for assistance to arrive. And they're here." Lily walked towards the woman, seeing Ev approaching her customers and sending them out through the kitchen.

"Susy Wright?" Lily stood in front of the woman, who looked up with a sneer at her. "You're under arrest. You can come quietly or not. That's your choice. But you will be leaving with these officers."

Old George hovered around outside the building that he claimed as his own. He knew that Lily and Bill were in the area. He had watched them carefully walk by him, a subtle nod from Bill the only acknowledgement that he saw Old George.

Richard, Stephen, and Timothy stood just inside the doorway. They were cautious not to be seen by anyone, but they agreed with one another that they likely had been  Now it was just a matter of getting Raleigh and Richard to somewhere safe.

Bill had been in touch with Old George, advising him that the hitman was still out there. They now had his picture and name, just not him. Richard had nodded, knowing that the next few hours were critical to them arriving safely home. He would take no chances with Raleigh or with one of his team.

Patrol vehicles screeched to a stop in front of the building. Old George faded back, leaving Richard's team ready to move out to the cars. Raleigh had crept to his side, not sure if she should have even though Naomi and Silver had nudged her that way. Richard's hand reached for hers. He knew that this was a dangerous moment, transferring between the building and a car. He just waited, praying for peace as to when to move.

On the move, Richard rushed Raleigh from the building. His team surrounded him as much as they could, officers moving in as well. Richard felt the bullet as it hit him, knocking him violently off his feet to hit the ground hard on his back. His head bounced once before he lay still. Raleigh screamed as her hand was torn from his before Timothy tackled her and had her down, his body covering hers. At a nod from an officer, Stephen moved in on her other side and between the two men, they moved her to a vehicle, Naomi and Silver sliding in rapidly before the car disappeared.

Timothy and Stephen were back beside Richard, Stephen's hands reaching to assess his friend. He nodded at a question from an officer before Richard was gathered into the arms and rushed carefully to a second vehicle. Inside with Richard, Timothy watched him carefully, a hand pressing hard on the bullet wound on his chest. Stephen worked away, assessing Richard's vital signs as best he could.

Bill ran towards the building, fear for his friend moving through his heart.

"What happened?" Bill turned in anger, not directed to the officers but at the situation.

"A sniper, Bill. We've got him cornered in that building." The officer pointed to the building directly across from them. "He's just not giving up. I don't know that he will."

Bill nodded, heading that way on the run. He had sent Lily to the hospital, knowing that one of them had to be there.

Raleigh huddled on a chair in the corner of the waiting room. She had not yet seen Richard but had convinced herself that he was dead. He had to be. She had been taken away too quickly for her to think anything other than that.  Naomi and Silver sat on either side of her, not moving for anyone, until they saw Richard's parents and brother.  Naomi was on her feet, heading towards them as they saw her,

Riley hugged her before he searched for Raleigh, His parents had already found her and were seated with her, arms wrapped around her.

"What happened, Naomi?"

"We had to evacuate the house this morning.  We had hidden down town.  When we were moving towards the patrol vehicles, Richard was hit in the chest.  Silver and I moved Raleigh out.  Timothy and Stephens were with Richard.  Timothy was out quickly, just to let Raleigh know that they'd get her back as soon as they could."  Naomi was angry.  "We were so close to getting them to safety."

"We know that you did your best.  You always do.  A sniper?"  Riley looked around as his father draped an arm across his shoulders.

"That's what we think.  Lily is here somewhere. She indicated that."  Silver stood nearby.  They were in shock and angry as well.

Raleigh was on her feet as she saw the charge nurse heading her way, Richard's parents beside her. Standing in the examination room, her whole concentration was on Richard.

"He doesn't need surgery? There was so much blood, Timothy said."  Raleigh didn't know if she had heard correctly.

"That's correct, Raleigh. We dressed the wound, stitched him back together, and started an IV with antibiotics and pain medications. As soon as that IV is finished, you can take him home." He frowned as Raleigh shook her head.

"Not to our home. It's a crime scene still, I think. I can go to the cabin. Only it's too isolated."

Rose's arm was around Raleigh as she blinked back tears.

"You'll come to us, Raleigh  You and Richard will stay with us for a day or so. It's what families do."

Raleigh turned to study Rose.

"Is that what we are?  Family?" She had prayed that they were.

"You have Richard's heart, Raleigh. And if I am reading you correctly, he has yours. Of course, we're family. And I have reached out to Abe. He will bring your parents and brother here. You need them."

Raleigh sobbed at that before she was across the room, an arm around Richard as she buried her face in his shoulder. He roused enough to wrap his good arm around her, a prayer whispered in her ear.

Reynold and Rose moved closer, a question on their faces that had Richard nodding. He slipped away to sleep, the pain medications making him drowsy. All he cared about was that Raleigh was safe and she was, there in his arm.

# Chapter 43

A week later, Raleigh set a plate of vegetables on the dining room table and stood back, assessing whether they had enough food. She felt Richard's arms around her and his kiss on her temple. Their love for one another had just exploded as he put it.

"Our families and friends are almost here, love." He didn't move, content to hold her. He had ditched the sling as he put it two days ago. The wound had bled heavily, but they thanked God that it had not hit any vital organs or major blood vessels. He was healing. That was all that mattered.

"That's good. I'm glad this is over, sweetheart. Bill and Lily will be here as will Andrew. We'll find out why, won't we?"

"I would suspect that we will. Bill did say that they had arrested everyone that was involved. People are talking now that the head ones are in custody. It will be a relief for all of us to know why. Have I told you today that I love you?" He kissed her, leaning back to grin down at her.

"You have. And I love you too." Raleigh hugged him before heading for the door. Her hand rested on the new door. Adam had chosen well, a steel door this time with an etched glass window.

Laughter and happy conversation wafted around the rooms. The families and friends who had gathered were glad for the couple that their adventure was over.

They wanted to know why, Bill and Lily promising to tell them just that when the meal was over.

Richard rose at last, heading for Silas. Silas had been waiting for that move.

"Okay, people. Let's spend some time in prayer. We have a lot to be thankful for."

When the prayer time had finished, Richard found Raleigh, perching on her chair arm and wrapping her into his arms.

"Bill? Lily? What can you tell us?"

"It's taken some work to sort it all out, Richard and Raleigh. There was a depth to it that we never expected to find. How well did you know Susy Wright?" Bill watched Richard's reaction.

"Susy Wright? I can't say that I remember meeting her at all. Raleigh?" Richard tilted his head to read the expression on Raleigh's face.

"Susy Wright? I don't recall meeting anyone by that name. Should I?" Raleigh was adamant that she did not know the woman.

"Her family comes from Riverville. She was Susanne Walters before she married." Lily watched Raleigh's face pale.

"The Walters? They're involved?" Raleigh shrank back against Richard, hearing her brother make a comment that he agreed.

"They are. They buy land cheap and then inflate the price very high. They wanted your forest, Raleigh. They didn't care about the cabin. They had been after your great-uncle to sell to them. He refused and had put in trespassing and harassment complaints about them. They were warned to stay away.

"Richard, you became involved through one of your clients. Henry West was a cousin who refused to play their game. You protected him from them before he moved away. He had no choice. They had threatened his live and the lives of his family.

"And Raleigh, there was another connection to this town. One of Hank Walters' aunts ended up in hospice care. She tried to take over her care. Your supervisor had to ban her from the premises. She blamed you without reason."

"It came back to her? I remember the aunt. She was such a sweet lady. How did she end up with them as family?" Raleigh's comment brought laughter to the room. "Are you saying that they were responsible for everything, even what the team felt was unfinished in their adventures?"

Bill nodded, his eyes on Richard.

"It was. She was determined to harass Richard and drive him from town just as she had with West. It didn't work. You were correct when you commented that it was someone from the church. She tried hard to take over various committees, and it just never worked."

"The hitman, Bill? Did you get him?" Timothy spoke up. He was worried that they hadn't and that he would come after Richard once more.

"We did. Unfortunately, it didn't end the way we wanted it to. He took his own life. He has a long list of crimes that he would have faced justice for." Andrew spoke up, knowing that there was regret that the families involved would not have the closure that they needed and deserved

Richard was silent before he began to pray. His prayer raised them right to the throne of God, thanking Him for the protection that he had provided for them. He ended with his usual "I love You."

"Who decided that they had to marry?" This was a question that had always troubled Riley.

"Susy did. She's not saying why. I don't know that she ever will." Andrew spoke up.

"Vengeance or hatred towards them, more than likely." Timothy was nodding at he spoke.

Raleigh reached to start the dishwasher that evening, her thoughts on what Bill and Lily had said. She was glad it was all over. There was still the lingering doubt that it was.

"Okay, love?" Richard set away the food before he hugged her.

"I am. I'm glad it's finally over, Richard. Did we really go through that?" She wrapped her arms around him, feeling loved and cherished.

"We did. I hated that we did. I hated that part of what the team went through was because of me. But if we hadn't, I would not have found the love of my life." He kissed her, moved away, and came back for another kiss.

———

"Richard? What do we do now?" Raleigh eventually asked, her cheeks rosy from his kisses.

"We go forward, love, as God wills that we do. He protected us in ways that we may never know. It's what He does."

"He does." Raleigh paced away from him before she spun and was back in his arms. "Thank you for being who you are, my protector."

# *Epilogue*

Six months later, Richard watched as Raleigh ran towards him, happiness flowing all around her. She leapt for him, her arms around his neck, knowing that she would just be wrapped into his arms.

"Happy, love?" Richard grinned down at her as he turned her towards their home.

"I am. I put in my resignation today to the hospice. I just can't work there any more knowing what they did." Her arms were wrapped around Richard just as his were around her.

"You're sure?" At her nod, he knew that she had made the right decision. "You don't need to rush to find something else."

"I think that I need some time. Going through what we did has changed me and changed my perspective on life. I'm thinking of going back to school, but I have no idea what to study."

"We'll pray about it, love. That's not a problem whatsoever. I'm kind of enjoying having you at home."

She grinned up at him, still amazed at his height.

"Your mom wants us to come for dinner tomorrow night. I told her that we can't."

"We can't? Did I forget something?" Richard was puzzled. He didn't think he had forgotten something.

"We do. We're going away for the weekend, finding that cabin out in the woods where no one will find us." Raleigh ran for the house, her laughter floating behind her.

Richard shook his head, his own laughter filling the air before he ran after her.

"We need to do this. We have been in court and under that cloud for months now. The trials are finished. We're free to go on with our lives." Raleigh paused on the back porch. "I made the reservations a week ago. I thought that I told you."

"You likely did. I was wrapped up in training and worrying about you." Richard hugged her once more before he moved towards the house. "Thank you, Raleigh."

Raleigh watched him disappear into the house. Their love for each other had grown more and more each day. They were parts of a whole. Everyone told them that, happy that they were together.

*Thank you, Lord, for bringing Richard into my life. I would be lost without my protector. And thank you for protecting both of us and protecting our team. Without Your hand over us, we would not have survived. You led in all things with us. And as Richard says, love You.*

Richard watched Raleigh, his own thanks rising. Raleigh was his heart. He would be lost without her. No matter what they faced in the future, they would move through it together, hand in hand, their prayer keeping themselves and whoever it was that was involved safe under the protection of God.

Thank you for choosing to read Richard and Raleigh's story, the last in the His Protectors series. This series dealt with God's protection on us. He never leaves us. He never forsakes us. God allows events and happenings in our lives but He works to increase our faith in Him through it all. When life gets busy, it is easy to forget that. We need to trust Him no matter what we are doing or where we find ourselves.

Once more, characters have decided to walk into this story. Abe and his team's stories are in *His Guardians.* Noah and Adam and that group of friends are found in *His Warriors.* Bill and Cora's story is *Hidden in the Hollow.* Frankie and Deidre is *The Storm,* part of the *Haven of Rest* series. Dave and Rylee had their adventure in *A Touch of His Garment.* Bill and Cora's story is *Hidden in the Hollow.* Andrew and Phoebe tell their story in *The Potter's Hands.* Silas and Madigan is *Strong Courage.*

I have enjoyed finally telling the stories of this team. They have appeared in many stories, providing protection for those involved.

God bless each one of you.

Ronna


Website: ronnabacon.com